The

Candle

Giver

"What sounds like violins—like harps being played and a chorus singing from somewhere amidst the pine and birch trees offer reassurance as snow angels lie in wait and eternal love spreads its wings, reaching beyond the mountain tops."
The Candle Giver

The
Candle
Giver

BARBARA BRIGGS WARD

The Candle Giver

Published by Wheatmark®
1760 East River Road, Suite 145
Tucson, Arizona 85718 USA
www.wheatmark.com

In cooperation with:
The Maggie O'Shea Company
P.O. Box 627
Ogdensburg, New York 13669 USA
www.barbarabriggsward.com

Cover illustration © 2015 Suzanne Langelier-Lebeda: SuzanneLebeda.com

ISBN: 978-1-62787-290-4 (paperback)
ISBN: 978-1-62787-288-1 (ebook)
LCCN: 2015941643

Chapter One

OUT EARLY SHOVELING SNOW THAT HAD fallen overnight, Steve noticed Thomas's truck parked down by the barn. He decided to go see what the little man was up to. With his son Sammy getting married the next day, Steve knew how hectic it would be even though very few would be attending. Although he wanted to, Steve hadn't invited a certain someone. He felt it wouldn't be the right time. He wondered when or if that right time would ever come. It wasn't as if he'd planned on meeting someone. After losing Abbey, Steve was certain he'd never feel again.

The day at hand was another one of those breathtaking winter days. The drifts on the way to the barn were up to Steve's knees in some places. A layer of frost made it seem as if the world was dressed in lace. A slight wind sifting through tree branches turned everything into a shimmering, swirling sight to behold.

Once inside the towering structure, Steve slid the door shut. He kept going until coming to another door that was slightly ajar. Peeking through the crack, he watched the sheep scurrying after the same old cat they were constantly chasing. As always, the cat had the upper hand. Moving through the granary and passing by the horses, Steve continued to the reindeer stall. He found Thomas busy spreading hay.

"No matter how often I see the reindeer, I'm still amazed by them."

"The herd is ready if needed, Mr. Steve. Come with me. I have something to show you. I feel it is time."

Following Thomas toward the back of the barn, Steve talked about the double wedding taking place in the farmhouse in a little over twenty-four hours.

"It's still hard to believe Abbey isn't here for Sammy's wedding. I'm thankful she got to know Cate."

"Did Miss Abbey know the other bride?"

"Yes. Maggie—the other bride—is the daughter of Abbey's cousin Ellie. When the kids were growing up, Abbey and Ellie would get them all together. Sammy and Maggie are about the same age. They kept in touch after college. The idea of a double wedding at Christmas was their idea. Cate and Maggie's fiancé, Teddy, are just as excited."

"Should make you happy that they chose to be married here."

"It does, Thomas."

"All staying at the farmhouse?"

"Only Ellie; her husband, Ben; and Ben's parents, Henry and Sophie, are coming. And yes, they're all staying at the farmhouse. Both couples are planning receptions at a later date so there will be plenty of celebrating."

"That's best with it being the holidays," remarked Thomas, walking into a space further back in the barn with small windows all around. "Being a dedicated sleigh driver that he is, I was aware Mr. Henry and his Sophie would be coming. Is your friend coming as well, Mr. Steve?"

A few months earlier Steve had sought Thomas's advice concerning that certain someone. Despite Thomas's words of wisdom, Steve hesitated with moving forward.

"No," Steve replied. Then he changed the subject. "This barn keeps surprising me. I never knew this space existed."

"It's out of the way, for sure. Not much use for it anymore."

"What was its purpose?"

"To repair or replace a certain sleigh if need be on Christmas Eve."

"What changed?"

"Turned out if a sleigh needed repair, it took too long. If it had to be replaced, time was wasted unloading and reloading. Any time lost was too much time. Now the team working at the other location has doubled in number to ensure a replacement isn't needed. But I kept all the tools, nuts and bolts, and leather straps in case of an emergency."

Switching on the lights, Thomas asked Steve to give him a hand removing a tarp from what seemed to be a rather large object underneath.

"Grab down at the bottom and pull the tarp up."

Taking hold, Steve pulled. Thomas did the same on the other side. As the tarp fell to the floor, an old wooden sleigh decorated in pine boughs and silver bells was revealed.

"This sleigh is for Henry. The silver bells were a gift from a good friend who shares his love of sleighs. The pine boughs were cut this morning."

Steve walked around the sleigh.

"It's obvious you've spent a good amount of time getting this sleigh ready. I can smell the wax, the polish. The leather seats are shining. They look new."

Steve kept walking around the sleigh. "Straps are as black as coal."

Guiding his fingers along one of the runners, Steve added, "I bet you used steel wool before polishing these."

Moving around to the front—pausing to take another look—Steve got down on one knee. "Amazing," he remarked, his hand going back and forth over reindeer carved in wood. "My guess is you are the skilled carver. No one could interpret reindeer better than you."

"Thank you. Though mighty, I consider reindeer as graceful as ballerinas."

"Well said. Ben told me about Henry's expertise in handling a sleigh and how he'd take orphans for sleigh rides through the back fields. Afterward, he'd bring them inside for cookies his first wife, Helen, had made. Henry made sure there was a gift for each child under the Christmas tree."

"He is a giving man."

"As you would say, genuine kindness is priceless."

Looking around, Steve asked about the additional space behind them.

"I will show it to you."

Going farther back, Thomas pulled burlap bags off windows, revealing sleighs lined up one after another.

"Why so many?" Steve couldn't believe what he was seeing! He felt like a little kid again.

"These are retired. Although Christmas Eve is but once a year, the journey is worldwide, in all sorts of weather, landing in all types of conditions."

"So eventually you need a new model?"

"Yes, and when that time comes, another sleigh must be ready."

They kept walking.

"This barn holds all but one sleigh," Thomas said.

"Is there another barn?"

"Yes," replied Thomas, covering the windows back up.

"Is it near?"

"It is back in the woods."

"There's another barn behind here?"

"Yes."

Noticing Steve's surprise at what he'd said, Thomas paused before telling Steve, "Miss Abbey knew. She liked going to that barn in the woods."

"She never said a thing."

"She realized it was not her place."

"I understand."

"I would like to take you there, Mr. Steve."

"The other barn holds that other sleigh?"

"Yes."

The thought of going there was all Steve needed. "Whenever you have the time, I'm ready to go."

"I have time right now. We will go by sleigh, Mr. Steve."

Chapter Two

THOMAS HAD THEM HEADING OFF IN minutes, forging through snow-drifts and around fences, up and over a bluff, and then straight into the woods. The landscape was breathtaking. Trees sparkled as if laced with diamonds as did snow—untouched—pure—soft as angora. A cluster of blue spruce seemed to reach to the heavens—their branches spread like angels' wings as a slight breeze sent bits of that glistening snow swirling. Farther in, against the frost-covered backdrop, hidden among the pine and birch, hints of a structure could be seen. As the horse pulled them closer, that structure became visible.

"I never would have known this was here if not directed."

"That's how it is supposed to be, Mr. Steve."

Once off the sleigh, Thomas secured the horse and led Steve toward the barn.

"Miss Abbey felt tranquility at this place in the woods."

Thomas opened a side door. "A place like this does that if you take the time to listen. Miss Abbey considered this her church in the woods."

Steve felt Abbey's presence as he stepped inside. He understood why she felt tranquility. The stillness was loud and clear.

"How was this built in the middle of nowhere?"

"To someone, it was the perfect location."

Walking through an archway made of stone, Thomas led Steve farther into the barn.

"Are reindeer kept here?"

"No. It serves another purpose."

Thomas kept going until he came to a space surrounded by more stone. Abbey's remark about this being her church in the woods was making sense to Steve. In front of them, down three wide steps, was an open area where frost-covered stone glittered in streaks of sunshine coming through stained-glass windows. A towering pine tree decorated in glass bulbs—so many glass bulbs in so many swirling, glistening colors—was centered in front of the windows. Standing there, Steve was reminded of a conversation he'd had with Abbey after she and Thomas visited the North Pole.

"The most beautiful sight of all was the area where the glass ornaments are blown. They took my breath away," Abbey had explained.

Looking at the tree, Steve understood.

"They're from the North Pole, aren't they?"

"Yes, Mr. Steve. Come. Sit with me."

Once down the steps, Thomas went over to rows of benches made of pine. He chose one closest to the tree and wasted no time in telling Steve his news.

"This is my last Christmas as the reindeer keeper. I intend to tidy things up and finish training a new reindeer keeper before I go. I will have other duties with the reindeer at home. I will miss you, Mr. Steve. You and Ms. Abbey included me in your family, and family is what Christmas is about."

It took Steve a minute to find the words. "I can't imagine you not being here, Thomas. You were such a comfort to Abbey. You became her best friend."

"You and Miss Abbey and your family will be in my heart forever."

If possible, the glass ornaments sparkled even more as the wind whistled around the barn.

"What will happen?"

"It's already happened, Mr. Steve. What you see in front of you is part of a tradition that took place in the early hours this morning. To carry on tradition is the purpose of this barn. That sleigh next to the tree was the first sleigh. That satchel on the seat was the first satchel used to bring Christmas around the world. We came together in a solemn ritual that takes place when Santa names his next reindeer keeper. I am pleased to tell you that he chose my son, Edmund."

"This happened today?"

"At exactly two o'clock in the morning, as tradition decrees."

"Santa was here? I never heard a thing."

"That's another tradition, Mr. Steve. The passing of the duty of reindeer keeper is to be performed in a secluded place and witnessed by only those chosen to attend."

"Is your son with you now?"

"He will arrive tomorrow evening. My duties end when the new year begins. Part of those duties is to introduce you to Edmund. Then you can get to know each other while I am still here."

"Whatever you need me to do, Thomas."

"There is one request. This only happens when a reindeer keeper returns home and a new reindeer keeper assumes the role, which is a rare occurrence. We ask that you—as the reindeer keeper's helper—begin to think about whom you would name as your replacement. Even if you are not sure, this will serve as a guide for Edmund."

"I think about that once in a while. Are there age restrictions?"

"Age does not matter. It is goodness and acceptance that is needed. Sometimes, no matter how old a person is, they never acquire either of those traits."

"This may be an odd question, but does the person have to be local?"

"Not odd at all, Mr. Steve. The person you select does not have to be local. There are ways they can be here in a wink of an eye and time would stand still around them, if you know what I mean."

"I do know what you mean. I'll put some serious thought into who will follow me." Hesitating, Steve added, "I will miss you."

"I will be with you, Mr. Steve. Those we love need not be visible to be felt."

It was silent for a moment in that most silent place until Thomas made a suggestion straight from the North Pole.

"I've been given permission to offer this enchanting barn to your family as a setting for the wedding vows about to be pledged. We have the means to transport the couples and your family. I am told sleighs and horses are quite romantic. It would be glorious, Mr. Steve, glorious!"

"Again, you leave me speechless, Thomas. While it is not up to me, I agree with you. It would be glorious—all of it would be glorious."

"I understand it is not your decision. I realize you will be unable to explain what this barn and the sleigh sitting in front of us represent. My hope is those gathered would be able to sense the worth of this place simply by being present."

"Eric and Sammy share Abbey's and my way of looking at life. I dare say Sammy's Cate does too. While I don't know Ellie's daughter that well and haven't met her fiancé, I sense from what I've heard they too are on the same page. I have no doubt the same holds true for Henry and Sophie. Once everyone's settled, I will make the suggestion we pay this place a visit. Then we can take it from there."

"Henry could drive one sleigh. I'll drive the other."

"It'd have to be later on this evening."

"I will be ready."

Steve went up to the sleigh sitting by the tree. "It's hard to grasp this sleigh was the beginning."

"I remember seeing it for the first time. We were excited, especially for the children. That feeling has never gone away. It's all about the wonder."

"Did you hear that?" asked Steve, distracted by something outside. "Was it the wind?"

"No. It was the horse telling us it is time to go, Mr. Steve."

IT HAD SNOWED WHILE THEY WERE in the barn but not enough to matter. With the wind behind them and the horse eager to go, they zipped straight out of the woods, up and over the bluff, around fences and through snowdrifts. Once they were back in the barn, Steve asked Thomas if he needed any help with the horse or sleigh.

"I'll get her brushed, give her a little attention," said Thomas, leading the horse to a stall. "But first I'd like to show you one more thing."

Thomas led Steve to a stairway half hidden by a wall. You had to take a sharp left to see it.

"This barn has places I never knew existed."

"It's not your ordinary barn," grinned Thomas.

"I'm getting used to that."

They took their time on the narrow stairs. Thomas waited for Steve in front of a closed door. With three panels of punched tin encased in seasoned mahogany, the door was like no other in the barn.

"Why is this door where no one can see it?"

"It's not meant to be seen by just anyone." While turning the brass knob, Thomas pushed. The door creaked open.

"It's warm in here," remarked Steve, unbuttoning his jacket.

"It has to be, Mr. Steve."

It wasn't too big of a space. Dormer windows were at either end of the room. Underneath one sat an old trunk. The other dormer window caught Steve's attention. "Magnificent view! I can see far beyond the fields."

"Being the tallest point, it serves as a watchtower on blustery Christmas Eves. That hook above the frame is for a lantern if needed."

"I would think a lantern has been necessary many a time."

"Indeed. A few times I've had to crawl out on the roof to guide the sleigh in."

"Has it ever been so bad that the sleigh couldn't land?"

"Christmas will always come, Mr. Steve, even when we think it's impossible."

Steve understood the truth in Thomas's words. Moving away from the window, the old trunk caught his eye. As he'd done with the sleigh meant for Henry, Steve moved his hands around it. Once lacquered, the pine boards were split in places. Worn leather straps hugged the sides.

"It'd been in the granary. When I showed it to Miss Abbey, she fell in love with it."

"It has character. Abbey admired character."

"She asked me to keep it for her."

"How did you get it up the stairs?"

"Perseverance, Mr. Steve. I told Ms. Abbey where I put it, but I do not know if she ever came here. I never asked."

"I can think of no better place for this trunk to be kept than where Santa is guided by a lantern on Christmas Eve. Something tells me Abbey made it up here."

A horn tooting nonstop could be heard. Steve checked his watch. "Time has flown by!"

"That happens in this barn."

"I'm sure that's Sammy."

"Go greet your son, Mr. Steve. I have duties I must tend to."

"Most important duties," replied Steve on his way back down the stairs.

Hurrying by reindeer, past horses in stalls, past sacks of grain, and around a cat being chased by sheep, images of Sammy as a newborn, a toddler, and then a young man flashed through Steve's mind like frames in a camera.

"Sammy's home, Abbey. Our youngest is home," whispered Steve to the wind—the magical, wondrous wind. Stepping out of the barn and into the snow, Steve headed to the farmhouse.

Chapter Three

IT WAS A FICKLE WINTRY DAY, with the weather going from sunshine to snow without a blink. By the time Steve reached the house, it was a blizzard. But it didn't quell his enthusiasm. It only heightened it. Whenever the wind whistled a certain way and the snowflakes swirled like feathers escaping from a pillow, his thoughts went back to a Christmas so long ago. We all have those Christmases. The ones that never leave us.

Steve was seven. With his father fighting in Korea, Steve tried stepping into his shoes, but that proved to be impossible. Steve's sisters were constantly quarreling. His mother was away most of the time, working. They had lots of babysitters. Because he missed his father, Steve asked Santa to bring him home for Christmas. And Santa did—very late at night as the wind whistled and snowflakes fell.

Now, going up the back steps of the farmhouse and through the door, Steve heard the commotion of family gathering. Not surprised, he found them sitting around the kitchen table. Eric had a pot of coffee going and a plate of spice cookies he and Greta had made were on the table for all to enjoy.

"Dad! I should have known you'd be at the barn. I was about to go find you!"

"I heard you tooting all the way down the driveway. Welcome home, Sammy! You made good time despite the weather."

"Nothing could have stopped us."

Steve embraced his son while asking if Cate had come in with him.

"Yes. She's showing Meg her wedding dress."

"I thought maybe she'd be outside taking pictures with all this fresh snow."

"That's on her list, Dad. The more snow the better."

"I remember how infatuated she was with winter that Christmas before your mother passed away."

"Cate loved every minute of that visit."

"Your mother did as well. Once in a while, she'd bring up Cate's remark about how spellbinding it was being in a barn full of reindeer on Christmas Eve."

"She was devastated when the photos she took of the reindeer didn't turn out. Mom later told me she wasn't surprised."

"Why?" asked Eric.

"She didn't say. I thought it might have had something to do with that odd little guy."

"Thomas?"

"Yes. Thomas. Is he still here, Dad?"

"Thomas is still here, Sammy. He's busy as usual."

"What keeps him so busy? There's only a small herd of reindeer and a few horses in the barn, right?"

"Don't forget the sheep."

"Okay, Dad. And a few sheep."

"Over the past few months, Thomas has spent a lot of time restoring an old sleigh for Henry. He'd like to take us on a sleigh ride."

"All of us in one sleigh?"

"Thomas has other sleighs ready and is able to drive as well."

"Does he collect sleighs?"

"You could say that, Sammy."

"I have a feeling Thomas and Henry will hit it off. They're both unique in their own way. Maggie told me Henry bought Sophie a ring only to have to wait sixty some years to ask her to marry him."

"Why the sixty years?" asked Eric.

"It's a long story."

Steve repeated the conversation he'd had with Thomas about Sophie and Henry.

"Their story is a beautiful story," said Cate, standing—listening in the doorway.

"It is indeed," said Steve. "Welcome home, Cate."

"Thank you. It feels good being here."

Hugging Steve, Cate wiped away the tears. Blending weddings with Christmas only heightened emotions.

The clock on the mantle chimed a new hour as Meg suggested they move into the front room. Carrying their coffee cups, in they went. Abbey's presence was apparent in every ornament hanging on the tree—some bought at a five-and-dime by a young couple who'd eloped when the soldier returned from Vietnam, some scribbled with crayons, some painted by a mother for her two little boys, and one, an angel, in place at the top of the tree in memory of a daughter who'd died at birth.

"Mom always said having the perfect tree makes the holiday. Now I get it. The tree is perfect when it holds a family's history of Christmases that have come and gone. I look at some of these ornaments and see Eric and myself at the kitchen table coloring. It was Mom. She was giving us a memory."

"You and Cate will do the same, just as Eric and Meg are doing."

"I thought I saw some new ornaments. They must be Greta's. I didn't recognize the scribbles."

"Observant, Sammy," laughed Eric.

"Remember, he is a film maker," said Cate. "He has the eye to see things others might miss and the talent to tell a story."

"I'd marry this young lady if I were you, Sammy."

"That's my plan, Dad. Through her photographs, Cate too is a storyteller. It's one storyteller marrying another, although," Sammy paused, his tone changing, "I seem to have run out of stories."

"What do you mean?"

"Any project I take on doesn't have to change the world, but it does have to offer the viewer a moment to take notice. I'm searching for that next moment."

"Like when you wandered through cemeteries looking for stories about life and living?"

"Exactly, Meg. Once that light bulb went off thanks to Mom's obsession with obituaries, it all fell into place."

"All the way to an Oscar," said Cate. "I keep telling Sammy that light bulb will go off when he least expects it."

"Sammy, you have the ability to sense when that's happening while most of us would see nothing out of the ordinary," said Steve.

"That's why my Sammy is so good at it."

"All I know for certain is I can't wait to make this talented photographer my wife."

Embracing Sammy, Cate whispered something in his ear. The two lingered until Cate made a suggestion. "I'd like to take some shots of everyone around the tree, unless you need my help with anything, Meg."

"We're set, Cate. Greta and Bobby are upstairs playing with the babysitter. Dinner is pizza from the restaurant with some of Eric's staff serving and staying for the clean-up so everything's in place."

"Are they bringing any of my favorites—your romaine salad with Gorgonzola? Any garlic knots?"

"I told them you'd be here, Sammy. They knew that meant extra salad and knots."

Once she had everyone situated around the tree, Cate began taking photos. Then Meg took a few of Cate with the family as the sun came out again. It certainly was a fickle day.

After spending some time with Greta and her little brother, Sammy went out to shovel. He missed the snow. It was the quiet, the beauty of it. As he cleared off the back steps, the image of his mother running down them came to mind. It'd been the day before Christmas Eve. She came rushing out the door without a coat or boots in ten-degree weather to welcome Sammy and Cate, Eric and Meg. It was quite a scene in the frigid cold—hugs, tears, and scrambling for luggage and presents to get inside the house. They were all talking at once. Funny. When looking back, it's almost always about the moments, not the gifts.

Finishing the walkway, Sammy noticed a vehicle coming down the driveway. The other bride and groom had arrived. It would be Sammy's turn to do the welcoming. Hugs, tears, and scrambling for luggage happened again outside the farmhouse decked in boughs and twinkling lights.

Chapter Four

"WHEN WE FIRST STARTED TALKING ABOUT getting married here, I never thought it would happen," remarked Teddy.

"This is much more than I imagined," said Maggie, eyeing the barn and fields and farmhouse, all decked out. "It feels like Christmas."

After shaking Ben's hand, Sammy gave Ellie a hug. Maybe it was the sunlight reflecting in the snow or the slight breeze or maybe it was Sammy being older—whatever it was—he noticed a kindness in Ellie's eyes that he'd find in his mother's.

"I think of Abbey often, Sammy."

"Mom was happy you stayed close over the years. You remind me of her more than I ever realized."

"I take that as a compliment. Your mother was a beautiful person."

It took a few minutes to get Sophie out of the SUV. With her cane in place, she held on to Henry's arm as they followed their son.

"Mom, Dad, I'd like you to meet Sammy. Sammy, I'd like you to meet my parents, Sophie and Henry."

"I've looked forward to meeting the two of you. I'm so glad you came."

"Sophie and I have watched your work. You are a talented young man. You get to the heart of a story," said Henry, extending his hand to shake Sammy's.

"Thank you. That means a lot."

As a documentarian, Sammy was infatuated by the couple. While talking to Henry, he envisioned capturing the old man on film. It might have been his beard. It might have been his wool hat with earflaps turned up, trimmed with fur, and pulled down to above his wild eyebrows. Or it might have been his eyes, wise yet laughing, or the way his wrinkles made him all the more intriguing. That same intrigue held true for Sophie. Even though she was crippled by polio, the woman's strength was apparent, as was her beauty, seasoned by time passing. With soft brown eyes, high cheekbones etched by years and hair mostly white, brought up in a bun, leaving stray wisps falling down on her forehead, she was definitely one classy lady. Whatever it was about them, Sammy felt their story was a story people would love to hear. He'd hold that thought for another time. The wind was blowing the snow in all directions.

"Let's get inside before we freeze."

It took a while to get everyone through the door and into the kitchen. Steve greeted them. Eric and Meg were behind him, doing the same. That's what it's like when family reunites.

"Your home looks like a Christmas card, Steve."

"Meg gets the credit, Ellie."

"Abbey was my decorating mentor," explained Meg.

"She had that flair. Abbey was always creating. I was the boring cousin."

"I've never found you boring," said Ben.

"Wait a minute, Ellie. Where's your son?" asked Sammy.

"Andy and his band had an opportunity to do a holiday tour through Europe. They start tomorrow night in Zurich."

"Andy's decision to go for it has turned out to be a good one," said Ben.

"Mom encouraged me to leave Wall Street and go to culinary school."

"And we've never been happier," said Meg.

"When you tap into your God-given gifts, all aspects of your life are enriched."

"True, Mom. Can you imagine if you'd never sewn a thing?"

"My hands are my instruments. Just as Andy plays the guitar you played at Woodstock, my hands play with thread and fabric."

"Did I hear that right? You played at Woodstock?"

"My band played back-up."

"Is that why Andy named his group The Architect?"

"It is," spoke Ellie. "Ben was the reason Andy fell in love with the guitar."

"You must be proud of him," Steve said.

"We are very proud. Besides being a pretty good guitar player, he and the others in his band have proven they can handle the pressure. But then, I might be prejudiced."

"I don't think you're being prejudiced, Benny. I think because you are an accomplished musician, you have a sense when you hear genuine talent."

"I don't know about my being accomplished, but you're right about that sense of spotting talent. I've heard many a guitar player over the years and I can honestly say Andy has it."

"So do you, Ben," remarked Ellie. "You remain Andy's idol."

"I can't take credit for his success. I only exposed him to the guitar."

"You also exposed him to what passion is," replied Ellie.

"On that note, I noticed another passion of mine when we drove in—that barn of yours, Steve. It's quite the structure."

"I thought that would catch your attention. We'll go down for a closer look later."

"And you can meet Thomas," added Eric.

"Thomas?"

Steve had talked about Thomas and the reindeer—to a point.

"The fact that we'll be near horses and reindeer on Christmas Eve makes me as excited as a kid," said Henry.

"You've always loved your horses."

"And you, my Sophie."

The old couple's love was apparent. When their eyes met, their hearts met as well.

"We were thinking," said Steve, "if the weather agrees, we could go for an evening sleigh ride."

"We've had our share of evening sleigh rides." Henry laughed. "This winter night, the sky will be clear—the stars will be out and the moon will be full."

"How can you tell, Dad? It snowed all day."

"It's in the wind, Ben. I feel it happening. We'll need to take two sleighs."

Turning to Steve, Henry asked who would drive the other sleigh.

"When you meet Thomas, you'll wonder if he'd be able to maneuver a horse and sleigh. Believe me, he's more than capable."

"Thomas can lead the way," said Henry.

It wasn't long before they were in the front room with a fire crackling and Perry Como singing in the background.

"Did you cut your tree down out back, Steve?"

"We did, Henry."

"I've cut a tree for as long as I can remember. I always think I'll never find a better one until the next year rolls around and I'm saying the same thing."

"I do the same."

As Meg was asking what everyone would like to drink, Henry excused himself. Sophie needed a sweater. Seconds later, Greta came into the room, dancing. Twirling in front of the tree, her long corn silk hair seemed to glitter as it swirled through the air. Her stature was that of a ballerina—her smile reflected a youthful enthusiasm.

"Such a pretty purple tutu," said Ellie.

"My Uncle Sammy brought it to me."

"Do you take dancing lessons?"

Greta slowed down. "No. I take riding lessons."

"Do you have a horse?" asked Ben.

"No. I have a pony, but I don't ride him. His name is Miracle."

"Such a nice name for a little colt," said Ellie.

"That's because he is very special. He is a pinto. Daddy and I found him in the woods."

"You found him in the woods?"

"He was cold and afraid. Daddy said he lost his way home and it was a miracle he was still alive."

"I think Miracle is the perfect name, Greta," said Ellie. "Is it a pony or a colt?"

"Greta considers Miracle her pony and that works just fine. Bottom line, Miracle is loved unconditionally. Eric thinks he was part of a herd of wild horses," Meg explained.

"Wild horses are around here?" asked Ben.

"Thomas told us they used to roam this region in great numbers," explained Eric. "We see tracks in the snow. Thomas insists they are wild horses."

"I'm surprised Miracle didn't run," said Sophie.

Eric further explained, "He'd sprained his ankle. He took to Greta. They've become quite close."

"I hope his mommy doesn't come and take him away. I would miss Miracle."

"If his mommy did, she would see how good you have been to her little one," said Meg. "Now your mommy would like to introduce you to our guests, Greta."

Taking her daughter by the hand, Meg went around the room. When they reached Sophie, Meg explained she was the woman who made the beautiful dress she'd be wearing the next day.

"And my cape with the shiny buttons?"

"Yes. Sophie made your cape, too."

Instead of saying hello, Greta gave Sophie a hug.

The little girl's expression of kindness filled Sophie's heart with joy. "I'm so happy to meet you, Greta. You will be a beautiful flower girl."

"Mommy is going to braid my hair."

"Perfect," said Sophie. "Your hair is perfect for braids. Now—I have a favor to ask of you."

Sophie whispered something to Greta, who then ran out of the room.

"This one?" she asked when returning.

"That's the bag." Sophie told Greta there was something in it for her.

"Can I open it?"

"Yes. This present has to be opened right now."

Paper went flying!

"Look! There are two things!"

"This is for your hands."

Taking a white velvet muff from a box, Sophie showed Greta how to use it. Then she took a matching velvet hat with earflaps and put it on Greta.

"I had a feeling if Henry had anything to say about it, we'd be in a sleigh at some point. These will keep you warm, Greta."

"Mommy, Look! I'm a princess."

With white velvet accenting a purple tutu, Greta went twirling around and around again.

"You are a pretty little princess,," said Meg. "What do you say to Sophie?"

Embracing Sophie in another hug, Greta thanked her for the gifts.

"You are welcome. But wait—I found one more present to be opened right now."

Seconds later, Greta was holding two snowmen made from bits of fabric.

"They are for the Christmas tree. One is for you and one is for Bobby."

"Can I hang them on the tree?"

"You certainly can," said Steve.

While Greta hung the snowmen, Eric and Meg brought in trays. One held glasses filled with eggnog. The other held china cups and saucers. As Eric headed back for the coffee pot, Henry came in with Sophie's sweater.

"Henry! I want you to meet Greta. She's hanging the snowmen on the tree."

"It's so nice to meet you, Greta. Your velvet hat looks beautiful on you."

Greta didn't say a word.

"Greta, Henry is talking to you," said Meg.

She kept staring at Henry.

"It must be the beard," said Sophie. "Henry gets this all the time."

Meg went over to Greta. "Henry looks a lot like Santa Claus, but you know the real Santa is at the North Pole."

"This is the real Santa Claus. I know it is."

"This is Henry. He has a beard like Santa."

"I know Henry is the real Santa, Mommy."

"How do you know, Greta?"

"My grandmother told me."

"When?"

"One time when she was talking to me."

"What did she say?" asked Eric, walking back into the room.

"She told me if I looked in Santa's eyes and saw them twinkle and he made me feel happy, then he was the real Santa Claus. Henry is Santa Claus. His eyes twinkle. He makes me feel happy."

"Henry makes me happy too, Greta." Sophie smiled and when she did her brown eyes—still so soft despite her years—seemed to twinkle as well.

When Eric's staff arrived everyone gathered around the dining-room table. Bone china dinnerware and a centerpiece of fresh greens and holly berries brought in from the woods sat in the center. Meg lit candles as Greta asked Henry to sit by her.

"Everything's delicious, Eric," said Sophie. "This explains why you've been so successful."

"Best pizza I've ever eaten." Ben was going for his second piece.

"Thank you both. Meg's educating our new employees as to what the restaurant is about has proven invaluable."

While stirring her salad with a fork, Sophie remarked how the young couple sounded like a perfect match.

"It hasn't always been like this. I'm surprised Eric stayed with me."

"Point is you didn't give up," said Ellie. "Getting through the hard times only strengthens the bond between you."

"I've always loved how you and Dad enjoy little things together," said Maggie.

"It comes down to the small stuff. Your father is my best friend," said Ellie.

Greta was growing restless. It was, after all, Christmastime.

Rubbing her stomach she told her mother she was full. "May I be excused?"

"Yes, Greta. We'll be having dessert shortly."

"Can Santa come and get me?"

"You will have to ask him."

"Santa, can you come upstairs and get me?"

Stroking his beard as if to hide the grin he couldn't stop, Henry replied with a bit of a chuckle. "I will be happy to, Greta."

"What a sweet little girl," said Sophie.

"She keeps us on our toes." Meg laughed. "I love the imagination at her age. She gets that from Eric."

"You have just as much to do with our daughter's imagination as I do."

"While I encourage it, she gets that curiosity from your side of the family, honey. I'm still learning."

"So you are a work in progress, Meg?" asked Sophie.

"When Eric and I lived in New York, I was an attorney—cutthroat and power hungry. Abbey made me realize how my parents divorcing when I was little still affected me as an adult."

"Both Mom and Meg discovered they held resentments toward their mothers."

"Abbey was a little further ahead in dealing with her feelings. She told me I didn't walk in my mother's shoes. It wasn't my place to judge her."

"Isn't that the truth," said Ben. "When I learned I'd been adopted, I was angry. Since my mother and father have become part of my life, I understand. I respect my mother's decision."

"Some decisions we parents make can cause havoc though generations," said Sophie. "I learned that firsthand. Abbey's advice was on the mark, Meg."

"Speaking now as a parent, I get what Abbey was saying to me."

Pushing his chair back, Henry added to the conversation. "I'm sure that's helped you in your law firm as well."

"I no longer practice law. After Greta was born, I didn't have it in me. I've turned to consulting business start-ups. My main focus is women struggling to get on their feet."

"How rewarding that must be," said Maggie.

"It is. Helping women become financially independent is gratifying. I never felt that when practicing law."

"That's because what you are doing is what you're meant to be doing," said Ellie.

"Without a doubt," answered Meg.

"May I ask a question? You can tell me it's none of my business and I will understand."

"If I can answer your question, I will, Sophie."

"I am wondering if you've reached out to your mother."

"Now I am the curious one. Why do you wonder if I've reached out to her?"

"Because you're a mother now, you understand being a mother is not easy. I can't tell you how thankful I am that Benny sought me out. I wasted valuable time thinking the child I gave away would want nothing to do with me."

Fidgeting with her spoon, Meg explained she hadn't contacted her mother because she was afraid.

"You might be pleasantly surprised, Meg. And if not, then at least you will know that you tried," said Ellie.

"Eric and I have talked about it, especially since having Greta and Bobby. I'm in touch with my brother who visits her so it's not as if I don't know how she's doing or where she is."

"I am not telling you what to do. I realize we just met but if you are thinking about it, don't wait too long, Meg. It is time wasted."

"I know that, Sophie. But it scares me. I wasn't a good daughter. I said some hateful things."

"From my own experience, I can tell you none of that matters. We all react and say things we regret. Bottom line, she is your mother. Everyone has relationships that need mending. That's part of living."

"Thank you Sophie. I value your wisdom and concern."

As soon as everyone finished eating, the staff returned. The table was cleared and coffee was served. Once apple cobbler was brought in on those silver trays, Henry went upstairs for Greta.

Chapter Five

"It gets dark so early this time of year," said Cate. "It feels like midnight even though it's only a little after six."

"And off we go on a sleigh ride! I can't think of a better way to spend the night before our wedding," said Sammy.

"Conventional we will never be. I think its romantic—snow, pine trees, sleighs, horses. I'm bringing my camera. Who knows what we'll see!"

"Dad said to take whatever you want out of the chest in the hall. Thomas will have plenty of blankets."

With everyone going except Bobby and the babysitter, the farmhouse was bustling. They took turns digging through the chest for sweaters, long johns, scarves, and mittens. Extra coats were in the closet at the top of the stairs. While everyone was getting ready, Ben and Henry walked down to the barn with Steve. It was decided they'd drive the sleighs to the house and take off from there. Sophie would never be able to make it to the barn.

"I'm in awe, Steve, to think that all of this was gifted to Abbey."

"It still hits me at times. The acreage goes on forever."

"Abbey's father never lived here?"

"He died a few months after learning he'd inherited it."

"The farmhouse alone is spectacular. The thickness of the beams, the wainscoting—it was built with detail in mind."

Whatever path Steve had shoveled in the morning was long gone. The echo of snow crunching under foot cut through the silence.

"For such a blustery day, it has turned out to be a spectacular night. You were right, Dad."

"It was in the wind."

"Henry, you sound like Thomas. You get to the point."

"Idle talk is for idle people."

"Almost lost a boot in that drift," laughed Ben.

"Not much farther."

In the moonlight, the silhouette of the barn set against the stars and snow was enough to make the three men stop.

"It's massive, off in a field," said Ben. "I can't imagine building such a structure. The cost would be phenomenal."

Once they were inside, Steve slid the door shut. When he opened the next door, he wasn't greeted by sheep chasing a cat. They were bedded down for the night. Although lights were on, they were dim. The moon streaking through small-paned windows illuminated the nooks and crannies and provided a path through the granary and into where the horses were resting.

"Is that Greta's pinto, sound asleep?" asked Henry.

"Yes, that's Miracle. I'm sure Greta tired him out earlier."

Steve kept going, leading Ben and Henry into the reindeer stable. Thomas had dimmed the lights even more. Steve understood why. Any of the reindeer could be called upon to journey around the world in a little over twenty-four hours. They needed to rest. Scents of hay and greenery drifted about, although no greenery was anywhere to be seen. Hearing a rumbling coming from the horse stalls, the three turned back around. When they found Thomas filling water troughs, Steve introduced Ben.

Henry didn't wait to be introduced. The door leading outside was open. He noted a lantern swaying from a pole. Even in the dim light, Henry was able to decipher what was out there. As he suspected, the pole was attached to the side of a sleigh—the sleigh Thomas had revived for him. The polish, the lacquers, the wax, the steel wool, and the aged wood all came at Henry as did the gleam and smell of leather. Sleighs defined the man whose hands were following the grain of the wood. He went to the back, to the other side, and to the front where reindeer carved in wood stopped him. He knelt down, never letting go. Now outside, Ben undid the lantern and handed it to his father, whose fingers were tracing shapes etched with obvious care. A few minutes later, Henry was back on his feet.

With his beard flowing in the breeze and a hand still holding on to the sleigh, he spoke to the little man who needed no introduction.

"It is a pleasure meeting you, Thomas. Without knowing me, you've told my story. It's about the sleighs. My life is about the sleighs—the horses, the cutters, miles through the back fields, with snow swirling and children laughing; a Christmas Eve journey with a wide-eyed little boy; the love of my life with me on horseback, in sleighs, in cutters."

"It's my pleasure as well, Mr. Henry. Friendship is not about time spent but the connection shared. I feel as if I've met you before."

"The stories we share are the connection. I feel there are more stories to be told, more stories to be remembered."

Realizing the others were waiting, draft horses were brought outside. While Thomas and Henry readied their teams, Steve brought Ben back to where the reindeer were resting.

"I wish I had the time to stay here and listen," said Ben.

"Listen?"

"I've been in a lot of old places. Many were eventually torn down because no one took the time to listen. I believe if they had, restoration would have been the answer. Buildings talk to us. The older they get, the louder they speak. Take this place, Steve, the squealing doors, the howling wind trying to get in, the plank floor creaking. Those sounds stay with you; they bring you back to a place and time."

"When I lost Abbey, I found my way back in this old barn."

"This place, with all its sounds and smells and memories, took you in and gave you comfort. That comfort came from years of wear and tear. I believe a child feels that when being cradled in a grandparent's arms."

"I remember sitting on bales of hay—sitting there, not saying a word—trying to find something to hold on to after losing Abbey. I found it as you described. The wind, the floor, the doors—they all offered me comfort."

The chiming of silver bells was their signal. It was time to go.

"This is a conversation for another time, Ben. We don't want to keep the sleigh drivers waiting."

Chapter Six

ONCE SOPHIE WAS ON THE SLEIGH, it didn't take long for everyone else to climb in. Blankets were passed around. Mittens and scarves were checked and then tucked in a little more. Ellie and Meg had made hot chocolate. Steve stored the thermoses under the seat he was sharing with Thomas. Greta was happy. She was sitting behind Santa Claus, between Sophie and her mother. Her hands were warm inside her velvet muff. She pulled the velvet earflaps close to her face.

"Take us to the North Pole, Santa."

"It's too busy there tonight, Miss Greta."

After making sure everyone was warm enough, Thomas asked Henry if he was ready.

"With this sleigh and team of horses, I am ready!"

With a nod of his head and a blink of his eye, Thomas signaled to the horses. They were off. Silver bells resounded over snowdrifts and around hedges. The faster the horses went, the higher the snow sprayed. Thomas knew the whereabouts of every tree—every fence and hedge. Once around a clump of maples, Thomas let the horses take over. Henry did the same. The field was wide open. The stars were dancing as were Santa's eyes. With his beard layered in snow and his eyebrows straight out, Henry pulled his sleigh ahead. Ben wrapped his arm around Ellie. Greta put her head in her mother's lap. But not for long. Thomas caught up, indicating he was turning. Henry knew to slow down. Using the moon as a guide, Thomas led them into the woods. Signaling for Henry to slow down even more, he wove that sleigh and those horses around trees crammed together in some places.

When they came to a clearing, they could see the outline of that other barn. The closer they got, the more visible it became. While the light of the moon did its part, the lanterns in the windows shed even more light into the darkness. With the sleighs side by side and the horses at rest, the sound of a distant train making its way through the night added to the moment.

The littlest one was the first to speak.

"Who lives here, Santa?"

"I'm not sure. We'll have to go see."

With her camera ready, Cate jumped out of the sleigh. "I can take photos, Thomas?"

This time Thomas said yes but asked Cate not to reveal the barn's location and to be reserved in the number of photos she took.

"The splendor would be tarnished should this be known to others."

"What's this place used for?" asked Ben. "I can only imagine how challenging it was to construct away from anything with no road in or out. It looks like it's been standing for centuries."

"'Tis quite old. It's used by my family."

"They visit, Thomas? I've never met your family. I never knew this barn existed."

"Quick trips, Miss Meg. Best to pull up as close to that side door as possible, Henry. It'd be easiest for Miss Sophie. I shoveled earlier but the wind has had its way."

"When they come again, Thomas, I would love to meet them."

Thomas didn't answer Meg. He kept directing Henry.

"Close enough, Thomas?"

"Perfect!" As he'd done once before on a winter's night, Ben helped his mother down off a sleigh. While it was a different sleigh, it was still a sleigh driven deep into the woods with the moon and stars shimmering. Sophie's cane again took some maneuvering. Henry again pushed away snow with his boot.

Thomas took the lead through the side door, through the stone archway. He kept going farther into the barn until he came to the space surrounded by more stone. Everyone gathered around him, looking beyond the three wide steps to the opened area.

"What is this, Thomas?" asked Ben. "Those windows—the stones covered in frost."

"Look at that Christmas tree," said Cate. "I've never seen a more perfect tree."

The towering pine with branches spread wide was magnificent—reaching to the haylofts—its presence the epitome of this season of wonder.

"So many glass bulbs! It's beautiful. Almost sacred," remarked Sophie.

"Do you mind if we get closer, Thomas?" asked Maggie.

"Please do."

"Can I sit by Santa, Mommy?"

Before Meg could answer, Henry took Greta's hand and led her down the steps. He tried getting her to sit with him on one of the pine benches but the sleigh by the tree caught her eye.

"Look, Santa. There's your sleigh!" Greta ran to get a closer look. "Your bag is here, Santa! Don't forget it!"

Henry stood beside her and told Greta he would never forget his bag.

"When do you go home to fill it, Santa?"

"When you are sleeping on Christmas Eve."

"It's hard to sleep on Christmas Eve."

"Close your eyes and listen to the wind. It will rock you to sleep, my little one."

"How did you decorate the tree, Thomas? It's massive," asked Maggie

"It's a family ritual," was all Thomas offered.

"I'd like to know where all those bulbs came from. I've never seen any like them."

Thomas didn't seem to hear Cate as he busied himself by the tree.

Teddy thought of it first. "Sophie described this place as sacred. I have to agree. I realize plans are in place and the work is done, but I see this as a backdrop for two couples saying their wedding vows."

As he came down the steps, Teddy kept talking.

"It's a thought. We could come back tomorrow, say our vows, and return to the house."

"The justice of the peace wouldn't go for that. Besides Meg, Mom, and Sophie worked so hard bringing everything together," said Maggie.

"Need not worry about a justice of the peace," Thomas said.

"Why?" asked Ben.

"Because I am licensed to perform marriages."

"No!"

"Yes, Mr. Sammy, and in any state."

"I've never heard of that," said Sophie.

"I have connections, Miss Sophie."

"What's the weather tomorrow?"

"It doesn't matter, Ellie. We have love on our side." Henry smiled. "And when you have love on your side, anything can happen!"

They sat on the pine benches for a while longer, discussing Teddy's idea and sipping hot chocolate. It didn't need discussing. As soon as Teddy threw it out there, it was a done deal. When you're able to envision possibility, the mind and heart become one. As he sat and listened, Steve remembered what Thomas had told him earlier about Abbey considering this place her church in the woods. Steve wasn't surprised. It brought her peace, just as the other barn had offered Steve comfort.

With wedding gowns, two brides, two grooms, sleighs, and snow, the logistics needed special attention. Teddy made another suggestion.

"Cate and Maggie can change into their wedding gowns once we get back home."

"I'd wear my dress," said Cate. "Wearing that dress when saying my vows to the man I love in this incredible place is more than I ever imagined on my wedding day."

"I agree," said Maggie. "Riding in a sleigh dressed in my wedding gown through the woods to such enchanting surroundings with you by my side would make the day even more memorable."

"Since the brides are happy with the idea, I think we have a plan," said Steve. "Do you foresee any problems, Thomas?"

Steve knew the answer. Once Thomas backed the plan, excitement took hold. As they were getting ready to leave, Greta ran back to the sleigh sitting by the tree. Reaching in as far as she could, her fingers touched the worn bag sitting on the seat.

"What are you doing"? Henry asked.

"I want to know what magic feels like. My grandmother told me magic is what you are all about, Santa."

"When did your grandmother tell you about magic?" Steve asked.

"She tells me all the time, Grandpa. Feel Santa's bag. It's warm, Grandpa. It's magic!"

It was warm! Steve looked at Henry who was smiling the biggest smile, spreading his beard even wider. Looking even closer, with the moon still shining through the window panes, Steve saw what Greta had seen. Henry's eyes were twinkling—dancing.

There was something going on in this barn hidden in the woods. But then, it was Christmas. Abbey's words were taking shape. Abbey's magic was at work.

Chapter Seven

ERIC HAD SPENT A FEW WEEKS preparing menus for the wedding day. He'd asked Cate and Maggie for suggestions. He wanted both brides to be pleased. The day would start with an early breakfast. Instead of a lunch, an assortment of holiday/wedding hors d'oeuvres would be brought in to the dining room to sit atop an old Hoosier cabinet. Ben and Sophie had noticed the cabinet right away. It was similar to the one in the kitchen at the camp run by the orphanage where they'd spend summers when Ben was very young. After the ceremony, they'd gather in the addition Steve had built with Thomas's assistance. Most of the dishes Eric planned on making would be served buffet-style. His assistants from the restaurant would do the rest of the cooking. They'd do the serving and clean up. Meg had spent hours decorating the space. She wanted it to feel a part of the old farmhouse. From comments, she'd succeeded.

The brides would disappear after breakfast. Meg had arranged for hairstylists to come in, along with manicurists. Sophie was thrilled. She'd never had her nails professionally done. She had no interest in a pedicure. The stairway was decked in pine and garland—enhanced by twinkling lights and silver bulbs.

THIS LAST EVENING BEFORE THE WEDDING was a busy one after they returned from the sleigh ride. They enjoyed snacks and Eric's hot spiced cider. He'd spent hours making cookies. Some recipes had been his mother's. She'd bake them for Eric and Sammy when they were little. Macadamia, oatmeal raisin, sugar cookies—platters of cookies filled the dining-room table enhanced by the candles in Abbey's brass candlesticks. Seasonal piano music played softly in the background. Cell phones kept ringing. Friends and loved ones were calling to extend their best wishes. Dresses were scrutinized. Suits were put out with accompanying shirts and ties. The grooms were reminded they'd be sleeping alone this last night before saying their vows.

Because the location of the ceremony had changed, they searched the cedar chests for even more blankets and shawls. Steve remembered a fur coat Abbey brought with them when moving in.

"It was my mother's," she'd told Steve.

While Abbey had pictures of her mother wearing the coat, she couldn't remember seeing her in it. Her mother had passed away when Abbey was fourteen.

Knowing Meg had the house organized, Steve decided to pay Thomas a visit. He asked Ben to go along, but with his daughter getting married the next day, Ben chose to stay back. Steve understood. With his son getting married as well, Steve felt the need to collect his thoughts. There was no better place to do that than where he was headed. It was so cold. The snow crunched with his every step. Zillions of stars seemed almost white against the onyx sky. About halfway there, Steve noticed a trail of what looked like footprints. Because the wind was quiet, they were still intact and led straight to the barn.

Once he opened the door, light from inside spread across the snow.

"Can't be," Steve muttered aloud.

Getting a closer look confirmed his first inkling of who had come before him. He found Thomas bedding down the reindeer.

"Thought you might be visiting, Mr. Steve."

"Tomorrow will be more hectic than usual for a Christmas Eve. I thought if we needed to talk about tomorrow night, we should do it now."

"I am running behind. I have not checked the winds or snow predictions."

"It's quiet outside. But then, it's winter."

"Of all the stops over so many years, this one—this year—is the most important. Because this is my last Christmas Eve, I would like it to be without delay."

"Whatever you need me to do, I'm here for you."

"Thank you, Mr. Steve. The reindeer are ready, as are the decorations and the tree. I can do nothing about the weather but be prepared for anything."

"Do I come at the usual time?"

"When you are drawn to the window by colorful sparkles, it will be time."

"While I'm looking forward to meeting your son, I'll never forget you, Thomas."

"I will be but a blink away. Edmund can bring you for a visit at any time."

"I'd like that. Abbey enjoyed every moment of hers."

"That she did, Mr. Steve. She spent extra time with Dancer."

"Seeing Dancer consoled Abbey when she needed consoling."

Realizing the hour, Steve said good night. Leaving, he turned and asked Thomas if Greta had visited earlier.

"Why do you ask, Mr. Steve?"

"I thought I followed her footprints."

"I have not seen Ms. Greta since the sleigh ride."

"My eyes must have been playing tricks on me. See you tomorrow, Thomas."

Steve shut the door and started back the way he came. But something was pulling him to that small space in the highest point of the barn. He stopped to get his bearings. It'd been daylight when Thomas showed it to him. After a few tries, Steve figured it out. It wasn't long before he took the abrupt left and there in front of him was the narrow stairway. Instead of being hidden in shadows, streaks of light fell about the area. Looking up, Steve could see the door decorated with punched tin was ajar. Judging from fresh snow on the stairs, he figured someone was up there. Being ever so quiet, Steve took it one step at a time. Stopping at the top of the stairway, Steve listened for any movement. Hearing nothing, he pushed the door open and went inside.

No one was there. Steve could tell someone had been there by the bits of snow still on the floor. Night gave the room a more secretive feel and more fascinating at the same time. Noticing the old chest was pulled out from under the window, Steve went over to see what was inside. But he never made it that far.

"I remembered I'd left the light on," said Thomas, hurrying inside the room. Going ahead of Steve, he pushed the trunk back in place. "All is taken care of, Mr. Steve." Thomas turned the light out and ushered Steve to the door. "Hold on tight to the rail."

When they reached the main floor, Thomas said good night and returned to the reindeer. It all happened so fast. Steve stayed by the stairs trying to make sense of what had taken place. He knew if he queried Thomas, the little man would talk in circles. He also knew it was late. Steve was certain his questions would be answered but not right then.

Once back in the house, Steve turned the kitchen light off and went to bed. Christmas Eve and a double wedding were near.

Chapter Eight

To Meg's surprise, the kids weren't the first ones awake. That's why she took her time—stopping to look out a small window on her way down the back stairs. What promised to be a glorious Christmas Eve was reflected in the early hour—with sunlight sifting through pines dressed in sparkling snow. The aroma of freshly perked coffee coming up the stairs told her Eric was already creating the wedding breakfast.

"The only time we hire a babysitter to stay the night and get up with the kids and they sleep in," Meg joked, giving Eric a hug..

"They'll need all the rest they can get with the wedding and Santa Claus coming."

"I need coffee, honey!"

"It's set up on the table by the bay window."

Meg walked over. "So many varieties." She selected her favorite and filled a cup.

"Owning a restaurant has its benefits."

"Could your wife order a bagel for after her shower?"

"I'll have it ready!"

With her arms around her husband, Meg whispered, "I love you, Eric. You've shown me what happiness is."

"Without your support, my love, I would be nothing. You are my happiness."

Sharing a kiss, the two lingered a little longer. Then Meg ran up to shower while Eric continued with the preparations.

Reaching for the pepper, he didn't notice he had company until hearing the clanging of coffee cups. Turning around he discovered Henry and Sophie.

Greeting them with a hug, Eric explained, " You'll find an assortment of flavors. The same goes for the juice."

"Sounds like you've done this before," joked Henry.

"Lucky for us, the catering keeps expanding."

"Well, something smells delicious."

"Breakfast is underway, Sophie. Thanks to you, I've included jam tarts."

"Oh you didn't have to."

"But I did. I'm glad you suggested them. It adds to the presentation when a family favorite is part of the meal."

"I knew this old nose smelled jam tarts. There's nothing more delicious that a piping hot jam tart," said Henry.

"You've eaten your share over the years." Sophie smiled. The two poured their coffees while the conversation continued.

"Let's hope I've done your tarts justice."

"Henry can be the judge of that!"

"From the aroma, I think you've nailed them, Eric."

It wasn't long before everyone was up. Sammy and Teddy ate in the summer kitchen, away from their brides-to-be. Eric kept the croissants, jam tarts, cinnamon French toast, omelets, and whatever else on the menu flowing. As planned, the hair stylists and manicurist arrived at ten. Cate and Maggie disappeared, along with Ellie. Sophie and Greta followed once Greta finished her cereal. Meg again proved to be an organizer right down to cancelling the justice of the peace. Thomas would be marrying the couples.

After eating, Steve and Ben went outside to shovel. The plan was to have the sleighs in front of the house by two-thirty. They would leave for the woods no later than three. The couples had discussed the journey. They'd ride together with Thomas driving and Steve sitting next to him. Neither groom would see their bride's gown until just before the vows were said. It was all planned. It was going like clockwork until it started spitting snow and the wind turned, coming from the north.

Having shoveled the walkway, Steve rejoined Ben who was clearing the snow off the steps "Feels like a good storm's not far off."

"Our winters are like yours, Steve. I think you're right."

The two set off to the barn to talk to Thomas. On the way, Steve remarked how intrigued Sammy was with Sophie and Henry.

"They're from a different generation. My parents are tough. They are survivors. You'd never know the sadness my mother holds inside."

"Sadness?"

Ben talked about Sophie losing her parents when a young teen and ending up in an orphanage and how just recently remembering having a sister."

"No family member would take her?"

"Because her father was Canadian, they lived in Canada. Her mother was American. Mom was brought back to the States after the accident. No one on either side of the family would adopt her so she was placed in the orphanage."

"From what Ellie told me, I thought she was an only child."

"Mom doesn't talk about it, except to my father. She was in shock after her parents died. She built up a wall in her mind to block any memories she had. Since marrying my father, that wall is coming down. He tells me how much she misses the sister she barely remembers. Her name was Lily. She was a few years younger than Mom. She admits there may be other siblings. But she doesn't remember."

"It seems with today's technology you could find Lily or whatever happened to her."

"I've mentioned that to my dad. He tells me they've discussed the option but Mom is hesitant. When I learned I was adopted I wanted answers right then. I was an adult discovering my life had been a lie. I began to study people as they passed me by, wondering if I was related to them. But Mom grew up knowing she'd lost her parents. She found a home in that orphanage."

"And it's a generation where their lives weren't plastered out in the universe for all to see. They were quite private. And to this day that's what they prefer," Steve said.

"I get a sense she wants whatever might happen to take its course so that's where we've left it."

They found Thomas brushing the reindeer. Steve brought up their concerns about the weather.

"We could go back to holding the ceremony at the house."

"Disappointment on a wedding day is not a good omen, Mr. Steve. We will leave for the woods as planned but get out of there a bit earlier. It's tonight that worries me."

Thomas got up and asked them to follow him. He led them back to an open area. With what sun there was sneaking through the clouds, the strands of silver bells adorning sleighs and horses were sparkling. Fresh boughs secured around both of the sleighs filled the barn with the scent of Christmas. White textured wool seats and blankets were in place, as were lanterns accented in holly and red berries.

"You've set the stage for what I am sure will be an incredible day."

"I had a little help, Mr. Steve."

Ben didn't question who did the helping. He was too busy getting a closer look at what Thomas had done.

"The detail you've included will convince Maggie all the more that this is where she was meant to be."

"What you see is just the beginning."

Understanding what else Thomas had to take care of, Steve suggested to Ben they get back to the house. Confirming times, they parted ways as those spits of snow kept coming down.

With help from Eric's staff, the kitchen was back in order. Silver trays full of cookies and more tarts were in place on the old Hoosier cabinet. They turned on the tree lights and put presents underneath the tree.

Right on time, two radiant brides and one excited flower girl came down the front stairs in stunning gowns created by Sophie. Maggie was dressed in satin. Cate had chosen velvet. Both would be wearing long fur cloaks. Sophie had included loose-fitting hoods. She'd discussed hairstyles with both brides-to-be when designing them.

Standing by the stairs, Steve and Ben were overwhelmed when seeing the two young women—so beautiful—so very beautiful.

While embracing his daughter, glimpses of her growing up came to mind. Time seemed a blur as Ben told Maggie how much he loved her, "You take my breath away."

Composing herself, Maggie thanked her father—then hugged him even tighter.

Steve couldn't find words to describe what he was feeling. Cate understood.

"I too am thinking of Abbey. I thank you both for Sammy. He is the love of my life."

"Abbey used to tell me how pleased she was that Sammy had found you. I'm sure she is as overjoyed as I am today. Your happiness is as apparent as your beauty."

After hugging Cate, Steve made a point of telling Greta how beautiful she looked.

"I have been to many weddings, but I have never seen a more stunning flower girl."

"Thank you, Grandpa. Watch my dress when I twirl."

As soon as Greta started twirling, sleigh bells could be heard. Henry and Thomas were waiting. It was time for the wedding procession into the woods.

Chapter Nine

Dressed in a pinstripe tuxedo hidden underneath a black wool coat, with boots and a hat with earflaps, Thomas accompanied the brides to their sleighs. By the look on his face, it was evident he was taking this responsibility quite seriously. A few hours earlier, he'd cleared away the snow—even put a whisk broom to the wool seats and blankets. When the time came to hand Cate and Maggie over to their soon-to-be spouses, Thomas felt a bit flushed when the brides took turns kissing him on the cheek. It was a moment enriched with velvet and satin as snow being moved off branches sparkled about the landscape.

Sammy and Teddy were waiting to help Cate and Maggie get situated. Both were so overtaken by the sight of the two stunning brides that Thomas had to give them each a nudge. Ben escorted Sophie on one arm and Ellie on the other. Steve carried Greta. Eric and Meg followed behind.

"I'm glad we decided to leave Bobby with the sitter. He would have been all over the place."

"No doubt about that, Meg. We would have missed most of the ceremony."

"I want to ride with Santa again, Mommy."

"Santa is waiting for you, honey."

"I think we'll be busy enough with our little flower girl," laughed Eric.

Sitting in the sleigh with the wind moving his father's beard and his eyes dancing, Ben had a brief moment when he thought he too was looking at Santa Claus, even though Henry wasn't dressed in red.

"Pull those blankets around you," said Thomas.

Everyone bundled up. Minutes later, they were heading to the woods on the day before Christmas in anticipation of two couples saying their wedding vows. The journey was even more breathtaking than before. Whispering to Maggie, Cate wished she had her camera.

Lanterns hanging in the trees turned the woods aglow. From a distance, the barn with lanterns in the windows could be seen along with hedges and pines surrounding the structure. With the snow gently falling and love in the air, it was marvelous to behold.

"Thomas. What a sight!"

"It has to be, Mr. Steve."

Once inside, everyone could see how busy Thomas had been hanging even more lanterns. The haylofts were illuminated. Clusters of trees surrounding the benches were decorated with those glistening glass bulbs. Branches of blue spruce and balsam adorned in pinecones and holly hung between the windows.

Ben was the first to notice. "It's warm in here."

"It has to be, Mr. Ben."

Ben understood there was no use in asking how.

Cate and Maggie, along with Meg and Greta, were escorted to a small room off to the side. It was spotless. Poinsettias and more evergreen wreaths had replaced the tools and cans of lacquer. Thomas had thought of everything—a mirror, hairbrushes, bottles of water—anything a five-star hotel would furnish was at their fingertips.

Sammy and Teddy waited in yet another room. It was smaller with everything in place. Waiting for the ceremony to begin next to where he was standing, Henry took a closer look at the old sleigh with the satchel sitting on the seat.

"I've never seen a sleigh built like this, Thomas."

"'Tis old, Mr. Henry."

"It has to be. Not because of the pegs keeping it together but the shape, the wood used, and those runners. This is a magnificent sleigh. Where did you find it?"

"A family member."

"Is it still used?"

"Hasn't been for years."

"The seats look brand-new."

"They were hand-sewn, Mr. Henry. It makes a difference."

"I bet it could beat any sleigh made today."

"I agree."

"The satchel catches my eye," said Sophie. "I think Greta described it best when she said it is Santa's. It's big enough. Looks durable. What's the material?"

"Feels like a soft leather, Miss Sophie. On occasion I wipe it clean with a dry cloth."

"I can tell it's made well by the way it sits on the seat. Did a family member make that too?"

"I am told, yes. A jolly one at that, Miss Sophie."

"So intriguing, Thomas. This whole place is intriguing."

"Indeed it is, Mr. Henry."

Bells ringing announced the brides were ready. Once the grooms were in place, Thomas nodded. It was time.

The door opened. Greta was the first to appear looking angelic in velvet. Walking toward the old sleigh, she dropped white rose petals from a basket Abbey had used when clipping flowers in the summer time. The wind pushing through the pines sounded more like Celtic harps being strummed as Maggie and Ben appeared. Steve and Cate followed. Both brides were radiant. Both held bouquets of white lilies wrapped in satin ribbons with sprigs of evergreen and small pinecones.

As Steve led Cate toward the steps, a conversation he'd had with Abbey came to mind. It was their first Christmas in the farmhouse. Opening a box, she'd found the boys' stockings lying on top.

"I can still see you sitting by the window, knitting late into the evening, in a hurry to have the stockings ready for Santa. Why is it, Abbey, that when your kids are young, you think they will be young forever?"

"I think it's because you're so busy you don't notice the clock ticking," she'd replied.

"The clock keeps ticking my love," thought Steve, leading Cate down the steps. "Sammy's bride is radiant, Abbey. She's holding on to my arm. She's smiling, Abbey—a beautiful smile. How blessed we are."

Pausing after the last step, Steve took a second to take in the moment, then he escorted the bride to the groom. "Your mother and I wish you and Cate everlasting joy."

"Thanks, Dad. You and Mom have given us an example to follow."

Taking Cate's hand, Sammy turned toward Thomas just as Ben was giving Maggie a hug.

"Love you, sweetheart."

"Love you too, Dad." Maggie took Teddy's hand.

With everyone in place—with white rose petals all around—the moment had arrived. Standing straight and sure, Thomas began the ceremony. It might as well have been taking place in the most glorious of cathedrals for the spirit present in that barn in the woods was unmistakable. Vows of love, honor, and respect were taken and rings were exchanged. Steve took photos. Cate had given him quick instructions.

"I now pronounce you husband and wife," said Thomas, not once but twice, as the wind kept the pines strumming.

Cheers filled the barn to the rafters as everyone shared hugs and kisses. Greta danced about, emptying the basket of petals around the old sleigh with the satchel sitting on the seat. White doves seemed to come from nowhere. They circled the barn and sang as Thomas announced one more surprise.

"In honor of this jubilant occasion, I invite you to enjoy a toast to the couples."

Pulling back an old door hidden behind the tallest tree, Thomas revealed a table dressed in a lace tablecloth. In the center sat a punch bowl. It was full. Slices of fruit were floating on top. Jam tarts sat on a plate.

"That's Mom's tablecloth, isn't it?"

"It most certainly is, Mr. Eric. Your father made the suggestion."

Doves kept singing as toasts in long-stemmed glasses were offered.

Thomas had even thought of a special glass for Greta for her own special punch.

"How did you get all this together in such a short time, Thomas?"

"I had help, Miss Sophie."

"That's the kind of help to have."

Thomas smiled as he checked the punch bowl. Aware of the shift in the weather, he kept an ear to what was happening. Spritz of snow had turned into a light snowfall. With the busiest night of all hours away, Thomas soon suggested they start back.

"We'll continue the celebration at home," said Steve.

Brides bundled up in cloaks. Coats and scarves were sought. Steve took a few photos of the tree and sleigh, of smiling faces and festive decorations that belonged on a magazine cover.

"Need help turning the lanterns off, Thomas?"

"No, Mr. Steve. They will be left on. I suspect their light will be needed."

"Before we leave, I want to thank you for all you've done for my family today. And if I didn't tell you, Thomas, you look terrific in your finery."

"Thank you, Mr. Steve."

Thomas kept going. Not showing emotion was getting harder to do.

Sleighs and horses were brought to the front of the barn as the wind blew. The husbands escorted their brides. Once Sophie was situated and Greta was in place behind Santa, Thomas turned to Henry.

"Follow closely, Mr. Henry."

Thomas led the way around trees looking more like eerie shadows in the darkness. Even with the lanterns, the denseness kept them maneuvering at a snail's pace. Reaching the edge of the woods, Thomas slowed down to wait for Henry.

"We'll make better time now, Mr. Henry. It's wide open all the way to the fence line."

"Good thing we had the lanterns."

"What few stars there are will help lead us the rest of the way home," said Thomas, distracted by Greta pointing over her shoulder.

"The white birds are following us," she kept saying.

Everyone was astonished to see the doves soaring along behind them. For a brief moment, even the moon made its way out of the shadows. Nature was sharing its blessings.

Ben was the first to notice the reindeer. That's probably because he'd sensed the same feeling years back. He knew what it meant. Thomas understood without explanation. He took a tighter hold of the reins. Henry did the same. He'd seen this phenomenon happen more than once on a winter night. Hesitating a bit longer, Thomas gave the signal. Off they went, hoofs digging in and kicking up snow.

Faster zipped the reindeer.

Faster soared the horses, leaping over drifts with such energy it felt as if the sleighs were off the ground. It seemed as if they were above the earth, mingling with stars as snow kept falling, and the reindeer appeared to hug the moon right along with them.

Then dashing past one field and then another, they went even faster until the fences appearing in the distance slowed them down. The reindeer disappeared. The farmhouse with its twinkling lights was on the horizon.

"It happened again, Mom," said Ben, helping Sophie out of the sleigh. "The reindeer showed us the way."

"And this time, Benny, showing us the way is wrapped around new love and seasoned love. That is indeed a reason to celebrate."

Chapter Ten

THE OLD FARMHOUSE WAS BUSTLING. AFTER Steve initiated a toast to the newlyweds, Ben followed with another. Everyone cheered when the two couples kissed under the mistletoe. Keeping in mind this evening of celebration was also Christmas Eve, Meg excused herself.

"I won't be long," she explained.

After checking her list and putting a few more gifts under the tree, she went upstairs. Soon the babysitter was saying good night. With Bobby in her arms dressed in his pajamas, Meg rejoined the party. Hanging stockings and putting Santa's letters by a plate full of cookies drenched in sprinkles would come later.

"We had friends tell us getting married on Christmas Eve would never work," said Maggie. "I can't imagine it any other way."

"Perfect cannot describe today," said Sammy with Cate by his side. Motioning for Maggie and Teddy to join them, the four raised their glasses.

"To all of you, to those unable to be here, and to my Mom, we thank you for your love and support. As one who tells stories, I am speechless."

Glasses were raised again as those gathered broke out in a round of applause for the newlyweds. Blending Christmas with wedding vows felt like wrapping joy with anticipation. When the food was served, Greta sat by Henry. She kept asking when he was leaving.

"Don't be late, Santa."

"Santa has never been late."

Looking outside, Henry hoped this wouldn't prove to be the first time.

The addition worked out as Abbey had hoped it would. Dishes were filled and refilled by those who'd come from the restaurant to help. Toasts were spoken and glasses were raised over and over again. Cate and Maggie had designed the cake. Two brides and two grooms did the honors when it was time to slice it. Then the fun really began. It turned out the couples had worked on a dance routine. It brought everyone to their feet as the snow kept tumbling down.

"I didn't know you had those steps in you, Sammy."

"Neither did I, Dad!"

"Our instructor told us Sammy was a natural!"

"Our instructor told Teddy to stick to his day job," joked Maggie.

ONCE THE EVENING QUIETED DOWN, STEVE sat in the front room with the tree lights on and embers in the fireplace glowing. He found himself looking at photos up on a shelf behind the tree. One particular photo sitting next to Abbey's parents' wedding photo caught his eye. It was of Abbey. She'd sent it to him when he was at Kent State. He told everyone about his girlfriend with the ponytail.

As the wind kept howling, a sudden brightness intensified, drawing Steve to the far window overlooking the back fields. Colorful sparkles were swirling over the land. Steve knew it was time. He headed out the back door.

There was so much snow. In places drifts reached to his hips. It was near impassable at times. With the wind howling and pushing the snow in all directions, visibility was limited. When he reached the barn, Thomas was waiting.

"Is that you, Mr. Steve? You are covered in white!"

Stomping his boots and brushing the snow off his sleeves, Steve asked where they should begin considering the storm.

"The snow is so heavy, Mr. Steve. In places it is freezing on. Somehow it will need to be cleared. But first, I must show you something."

Thomas led Steve into the reindeer stable where glittering crystals were everywhere. Fresh boughs of cedar and pine were wrapped about wooden posts and wreaths were hung in front of windows up high. Standing in the midst of it all was a most splendid Christmas tree. Wild berries and acorns were strung around its branches.

"Again, Thomas, you've created a most stunning sight. I don't know how you have time to accomplish so much."

"No choice, Mr. Steve. Tradition dictates what needs to be done, not time. But sometimes tradition is not enough."

"What do you mean?"

"Santa is behind schedule. The weather is dictating tonight."

"I'll get back out there and try to clear a pathway in."

"It's not just here. It's a wild night most of the way, causing Santa to ask that another sleigh be readied for when he arrives."

"Do you have the time to do that?"

"I have no choice. It will be ready. The children are waiting."

"Good thing you saved all those nuts and bolts."

"For certain, Mr. Steve. I need you to go up and put the lantern in the window while I work on a sleigh."

"I'll put the lantern in place and clear away what snow I can."

Thomas was on his way as Steve went looking for the hidden stairway. Despite the lack of moonlight, it didn't take him long. Drawing on what he remembered, Steve was up the stairs and in that small space in no time. Once he turned the light on, he found a lantern and put it in place as the wind seemed to howl even louder in this highest point. Noticing the snow outside piled high against the window, Steve realized that Santa would never see the lantern. He knew he'd have to climb out and clean the window off. It was frozen shut.

With great effort, he was able to open the other window. Pulling himself up on the sill, Steve wedged his way out onto the roof. The force of the wind almost carried him away as he held on to the window edge the best he could. He stayed there for a second, getting his bearings, slowly lifting his head, and adjusting his eyes. The snow was relentless. It stung his face. It came at him from all sides.

Steve knew if he stood up he'd be a goner so he crawled his way forward. The other window wasn't far away. It only seemed like an eternity. Once he reached it, Steve discovered the snow was half ice. But that didn't stop him. It was Christmas. Steve used his glove to break away the ice. It wasn't easy. He was almost airborne a few times, but he did it. The window was cleared. The light from the lantern would be visible in the storm. It was a little easier getting back inside.

Steve was about to go back downstairs when something on the floor by that old trunk caught his eye. Going over and picking it up, Steve stood there, staring. It was one of Sophie's little snowmen, one of the two she'd brought with her. Steve was certain. He remembered the mittens were different colors. There was no time to waste. Steve put the snowman on top of the trunk, turned the light off, and made his way down the stairs. As he shoveled, thoughts of that little snowman stayed with him.

In places where the snow was the heaviest, Steve did the best he could in the time he had. He knew Santa would be landing in the field behind the barn so that's where he spent much of his time—aware the wind would most likely fill it back in. In places where the drifts were so thick he didn't bother to try to get through them. He went around instead. Realizing time was flying by , Steve went back inside to see how Thomas was doing.

"Your face is as red as Santa's suit, Mr. Steve."

"I had to do a high-wire act on the roof. The wind is nasty out there."

"I've had to hold on to those window frames. Tonight sounds even worse."

"While the lantern's in place, I wonder if Santa will be able to see it."

"He's been told about the lanterns in the woods. He will use them as a guide."

"I can always go back out on that roof and wave him in."

"Time will determine that, Mr. Steve."

"How's the sleigh?"

"I have come to the conclusion that I shall never throw anything away. I needed one rare nut and bolt and I found the only ones I had saved in a glass jar. Because of that, the sleigh is ready to go. We will need to take it for a short run to be sure. It could prove to be an adventure out there."

Instead of hitching the sleigh to horses, Thomas brought out two older reindeer. He explained the difference.

"Horses and reindeer pull a sleigh differently. Santa once told me all they have in common are hoofs. It has to do with their girth. A reindeer is able to adapt quicker."

Even in the wind and cold, it took Thomas but a few minutes to hitch the reindeer to the sleigh. Grabbing blankets, Steve climbed up next to his friend.

"Once around, Mr. Steve, and then back we come. Much to do. Much to do."

Picking up the reins, Thomas instructed Steve to stay alert to any strange sounds—clangs or pings. They took off so quickly that Steve almost flew off the sleigh.

"Hold on, Mr. Steve. Off we go on a Christmas Eve!"

The snow was relentless as was the wind. It didn't bother the reindeer. Thomas said they'd be full of spirit after having been cooped up for so long and he was right. They surged over towering snowdrifts one right after another and every time, the sleigh held its own. Approaching the last open field before the fence line, Thomas knew they had the momentum so he pulled back on the reins and up they went, hurling through snow coming at them from all directions.

Steve tried keeping his eyes open but ice pellets kept hitting him. Following Thomas's lead, Steve drew his scarf tighter about his face.

Reaching the height he'd hoped to, Thomas loosened his grip. The reindeer reacted, bringing the sleigh back down through storm clouds. Using the lanterns he'd left hanging in trees and hedges and around the stately old barn as his guide, Thomas brought that sleigh down without a hitch. Prancing through the snow, the reindeer lifted one hoof in front of the other in sync with the wind.

"Not one ping or squeak, Thomas. That was an exhilarating ride. I can't imagine how Santa Claus feels going around the world."

"It's about the giving, Mr. Steve."

"Most definitely."

Jumping down off the sleigh, Steve added, "I'd say that rare nut and bolt worked."

"Most assuredly."

As quickly as he'd readied the sleigh, Thomas did the same when getting the sleigh back inside the barn and the reindeer unhitched and bedded down. He had to. Santa was minutes away. He felt it.

"I can go back out and shovel, Thomas."

"No need, Mr. Steve. My family will take care of Santa."

Thomas was all smiles. Steve sensed the pride Thomas was feeling.

Chapter Eleven

No matter how many times Steve heard the faint jingling of bells while standing in the barn on a Christmas Eve, he felt that wonder only believing can bring. This year while waiting in the barn for Santa Claus, Steve noticed there were three chairs instead of the usual two sitting next to the tree beside a small table holding Santa's pipe and now three cups of hot chocolate instead of two. The jingling was getting louder.

After motioning for Steve to stay put, Thomas approached the back of the barn, which was more door than wall. Taking a last look around, he slid the latch up and pushed with all his might. As the bells grew louder and swirls of crystals intensified, the door slowly opened. Snow came soaring in as the jingling stopped. A hush blanketed the night as Santa Claus stepped into the barn. Still with a smile as warm as summer, Santa approached the reindeer. Steve watched as Santa spent time petting each one while checking the might of their antlers and width of their legs.

In came the elves carrying packages they placed under the tree. Others carried a tray piled high with cookies. Soon all the elves gathered around Thomas. But this year was different. They lingered a little longer. Tonight would be the last time they'd gather around this reindeer keeper. Santa sensed the moment.

"Thank you, Thomas, for all you have done, not only for me and others at the North Pole but for everyone around the world."

Tradition took a back seat as applause broke out in that barn set off in a field. Steve was certain he figured out which elf was Edmund. He had that seriousness about him. Being the reindeer keeper does that.

Thomas called Steve over to meet his son.

Getting closer, Steve could see more similarities between the two. It was in the eyes. Just as Ben was certain old buildings had a language all their own, Steve felt the same about a person's eyes. Honesty and respect spoke as Edmund shook Steve's hand.

"I look forward to working with you, Edmund. It was with great pride your father told me you'd been chosen as the reindeer keeper."

"I am humbled, Mr. Steve. My father speaks with great respect of you and Miss Abbey."

They made plans to meet after Christmas.

While reindeer were switched, one sleigh unloaded, and a replacement loaded, Santa spent some time with Steve.

"Are you ready for Thomas's departure?"

"I won't know until I come down here and he's nowhere to be found, Santa. Thomas has become a good friend. There were times after losing Abbey when I didn't think I could go on but Thomas was always there."

"I once told Abbey she'd be leaving a lifetime of kindness to those she loved. I believe that kindness and her enduring love for the two of you have kept you both going. I am certain you and Edmund will develop a close relationship. Thomas has taught him well."

"Having just met Edmund, my instinct tells me he is as honorable as his father."

"Indeed," said Santa.

After switching a few more reindeer, Santa continued. "I was glad to hear the wedding took place at the barn in the woods. Thomas told me how the white doves followed you. Their presence is considered a blessing."

"That makes the day even more amazing. Were you aware it was a double wedding?"

"Yes. And I understand Henry and Sophie were able to attend."

Steve was about to ask Santa how he knew them. Then he realized Santa knows everyone.

"Excuse me, Steve. I must speak with Thomas."

Steve tried to figure out what was going on as Santa and Thomas went in to the granary. It wasn't long before Santa returned.

"Everything's set. Come with me, Steve."

Seconds later, they were sitting in chairs around the small table by the tree. The reindeer were the first to sense the door moving. Their stirring alerted Santa. He stood. Steve followed his lead. Glittering crystals were everywhere as the door opened and in stepped Thomas. He was followed by Henry. Thomas moved him along. Time was ticking. Once in front of Santa, Thomas stepped aside.

"Welcome, Henry. I still remember you as a little boy on your family's farm. How you've grown!"

Henry couldn't find the words. His expression reflected his surprise.

Santa helped him. "Yes. It's me, on my way around the world."

"But—"

"You're wondering if you're dreaming?"

"I must be. I'm an old man worn by years. I remember when I was a child I believed with every ounce of my being in Santa Claus. It was never about presents. There's something spiritual in believing the way a child believes."

"That's why I asked you here tonight."

"Asked me?"

"You did see those colorful crystals?"

"I came down for a drink of water. As I turned to go back to bed, a brightness coming from outside caught my eye. When I looked out the window, I saw what you describe as colorful crystals swirling all around. I noticed this barn all lit up. And next thing I know, I am here, talking to you. At least I think I'm . . . talking to . . . to you, Santa. I don't understand, though. Why me? Why am I here? Is this all a dream? Is it?"

"When you take orphans on sleigh rides—then invite them in to your home, you are giving a gift that can't be bought. Home is a place that dwells in our hearts. For many, that's the only place it ever exists."

"But so many others do so much more."

"So many others do so much more and sometimes for the wrong reasons. You never asked for a thing. You did it over and over. When you bring happiness to a child, you plant a seed of goodness. Walk with me, Henry."

Out into the night they went.

"I remember when you were a little boy you left me a note. It was lying on top of the cookies so I assumed you didn't want me to miss it."

"I don't remember doing that. I do recall leaving cookies and fresh milk every year with my brothers and sisters. Mom would bake oatmeal cookies the day before Christmas and we made sure you were left the biggest ones."

"The plate was bone china. It was always that same plate."

"That was the one fancy plate my mother owned. It'd been passed down through generations. The only time she brought it out was on Christmas Eve to hold the oatmeal cookies for you, Santa."

"Those were the best cookies, Henry. I'd always wrap one up and save it for Thomas."

"Thomas? That little guy in the barn?"

As the two kept walking, Santa explained Thomas's role as well as Steve's and Abbey's before him. He pointed out the reindeer were being groomed to become part of his team if needed. Santa knew Henry would grasp all he revealed and keep it to himself. Henry had proven to be an honest person since growing up on a farm run with little money. Of all the children, Henry helped the most. He'd also go out of his way to bring eggs to the orphans about every other day. Sometimes he'd bring vegetables from the garden. In his late teens, Henry went off to war and when returning took over the farm to keep it in the family and care for his ailing mother. Never once did Henry let on about his feelings towards Sophie. Not once over the years did he allow those feelings to cast a shadow on his marriage to Helen. He was a good husband despite a wild, unrelenting passion and love for Sophie locked away in his heart until fate stepped in long after Helen passed away.

The wind was still strong, and the snow kept falling as the two kept walking.

"What a story, Santa. I admit Thomas had me wondering. If anything, I found him to be quite loyal to the reindeer, to Steve. Now it all makes sense if one is of the mind to grasp hold of all you have told me. And I am one of those graspers!"

"I knew you would be, Henry. You once wrote me, asking if I'd give you my sleigh as a gift for Christmas. I had a chuckle over that request. You're the only one who ever asked such a thing."

"I don't remember asking. But I'm not surprised. Sleighs have always fascinated me."

"Realizing we share that fascination, I knew you'd enjoy sitting on the sleigh that will finish the journey tonight."

Santa motioned for Henry to climb on board. He hesitated. Even in the shadows, Santa caught sight of the marvel in Henry's eyes.

"I'll go first."

Once he was situated, Henry followed. They looked like brothers sitting there. In a way, they were. When you believe as they believed, it becomes a part of you. Greta sensed that in Henry. That's why she was convinced he was Santa Claus.

Sitting there, holding on to the reins, listening to the reindeer grunt, watching them paw the snow and seeing their breath curl about their heads and fade into the snowfall, Henry was struck by that wonder all around even as the storm kept on.

"If everyone could have a moment sitting in this sleigh on Christmas Eve, then maybe the world would be without war, without poverty—without selfishness. If only we could believe as we did as children. There's nothing more powerful. There's nothing more genuine, Santa."

"True, Henry. Yet sadly, so many are immersed in their own wants and needs. They'd never be open to such an idea. The faster the world moves the more distant from one another they become."

"That makes it all the more important to stay close to our beliefs, Santa, and to pass them on to the children."

"Again you are right, Henry. The children untarnished by life will embrace that spirit."

The ringing of church bells echoed in the distance. Despite the weather, they kept talking.

"I would like to ask something of you, Henry. Feel free to tell me no."

"What is it, Santa?"

"On a rare night such as this, with an old sleigh needing to be revamped to finish the trip, I'm apprehensive about getting it off the ground. I know Thomas and Steve tested it, but that was without the load I am carrying and a full team of reindeer. Would you follow me for a distance? If I feel the sleigh has what it takes, I will signal and then be on my way."

"You mean drive a sleigh up there through the storm?" Henry questioned with a little smile.

"Yes."

"But I've never driven a sleigh in that manner."

"There's nothing different driving above the earth than driving through the snow. The reindeer do it all. Just steer them clear of buildings and trees. They know the way."

"But the landing, I leave that up to them as well?"

"You do. It's instinct, Henry. Thomas has worked with the reindeer. They are groomed for the journey in all types of weather. Your belief will kick in. You will be astonished by the experience."

"You feel I am able to do this?"

"Besides Thomas, you are the only one I would ask."

"With you trusting me, I will be honored to follow you, Santa."

"I will ask Thomas to hitch a team to your sleigh."

"My sleigh?"

"The sleigh you drove into the woods. It is no ordinary sleigh. Thomas made sure of that."

Reaching under the seat, Santa pulled out a rather large satchel. Stepping down off the sleigh, he turned and waited for Henry. Then they headed back to the barn as more of those colorful crystals swirled about the most magical night of all.

Chapter Twelve

"Everything is set, Santa."

Thomas had filled the cups with hot chocolate and put a plate of cookies on the table. All Santa had to do was nod and Thomas would know he was ready to leave. Edmund followed his father to the back of the barn.

"Did you think I'd taken off, Steve?" Santa asked.

"No, Santa. I knew you and Henry had much to discuss."

Santa and Henry joined Steve around the table. While the two men talked, Santa opened the satchel.

"Incredible night, Steve. Incredible. Never in my wildest dreams could I have imagined this happening to me and at my age."

"You're never too old to believe," remarked Santa, pulling out letters held together by a ribbon.

"That has been proven tonight," said Henry.

"I'm still amazed. Funny thing though, I don't think Abbey was surprised. She sensed something about Thomas the minute they met."

"Thomas is not one to show emotion, Steve. Abbey changed him."

As Edmund led reindeer back and forth, Santa undid the ribbon and adjusted his glasses. Taking a sip of hot chocolate, he turned his attention back to Henry.

"You stated how in your wildest dreams you wouldn't have imagined this happening to you. I will read a few of the letters you sent me over the years. They reinforce the reasons why you are sitting here tonight. And about those letters—I could tell early on you possessed a gift for writing. Your letters stood out even when you were so young."

"Funny you should say that, Santa. I am a man of few words. I feel best when writing my thoughts."

Henry grabbed a cookie. Sophie would often mention he'd reach for something sweet when he got nervous.

"You wrote this when you were seven."

> *Dear Santa,*
>
> *My daddy coughs all the time. Mommy makes him tea in an old cup. I think he would feel better if he had a fancy cup like the plate my mother puts your cookies on. My brother Joe needs a new shirt. Mommy ripped two of his shirts so he could wear them after he broke his arm. He fell out of the haymow. My sister Claire burned herself on our wood stove. Mommy said she needs to go into the hospital but it costs a lot of money so could you take care of her? I know you have magic, Santa. I see it every Christmas morning. I'm okay. Please help me with my family. I love them very much.*
>
> *Your friend who lives in the old red-shingled farmhouse on Bunker Road,*
>
> *Henry*

As Santa folded the letter and put it back in the envelope, Henry talked about his father's old teacup.

"It was white. That teacup was white with a chip on the inside of the brim. My mother used it because it was bigger than the other three cups she had in the cupboard. She was convinced the tea helped him breathe. His asthma got worse over the years. He eventually died because of it."

"You were always thinking of your family, Henry."

"I don't know why but I felt responsible. My father loved his new teacup and a few days into the new year, a doctor's wife came by the house. She brought some things for my mother to alter. When she saw Claire she went home and told her husband. When the woman returned her husband was with her. He examined Claire. He made arrangements to have her treated and never charged my parents a penny. One night I heard my mother crying. She was relieved Claire would not be scarred for life. She called it a miracle. Santa, I knew it was you."

"The spirit of caring for others overtook that doctor. I'd like to read you another letter. You were twelve when you asked me for something special for your mother."

> *Dear Santa,*
>
> *Most guys my age don't believe in you. I don't admit it to anyone but I still do. I mean, there always has to be wonder and belief, Santa. I'm writing to ask if you could bring my mother a new dress. She's a real good seamstress but I would like her to have a dress from a fancy store. I would like the dress put in a box from the store and covered in white tissue paper. I would like it wrapped with bright wrapping paper and a big red bow. My mother never buys anything for herself. The twins will be graduating. They are the first to graduate from high school. My parents were never able to. So I would like her to look very pretty, prettier than usual.*
>
> *Thank you, Santa.*
>
> *Your friend who still lives in the old red-shingled farmhouse on Bunker Road,*
>
> *Henry*
>
> *P. S. My mom's favorite color is green*

"She looked beautiful at the graduation. The green in the dress matched her eyes."

Realizing he had to get going, Santa skipped to the last two letters.

"When someone writes to me, no matter their age, they write with their heart wide open. This letter is yet another example. You and Helen were still newlyweds."

> *Dear Santa,*
>
> *Imagine this! A grown man writing Santa Claus. By now I consider you my friend. You seem to understand my letters, what I am*

*asking, what I am feeling. It's been some year. My father died shortly
after I returned from the war. My mother was ill and none of my siblings wanted the farm so I took it over. That's when I met Helen. She's
from a good farming family over the county line. I married her, Santa.
Because I have been truthful in my letters, I will tell you I do not love
her in the way I love my darling Sophie. But that love can never be. I
will be a good husband. I will provide for Helen. But I will never forget
Sophie. Sometimes we have a love that is kept within our heart. I ask
that you watch over her, Santa. I ask that you keep my Sophie safe.*
    Henry

This time, Henry remained silent in the old barn on Christmas Eve.
Santa opened the last envelope.

"You wrote this after you and Sophie were married."

    Dear Santa,
    *I'm writing to tell you my darling Sophie and I were married
this past October surrounded by family and orphans who'd lived
with Sophie at the orphanage. Imagine that, Santa! At our age, so
blissfully in love!*
    *Merry Christmas, Santa. Merry, Merry Christmas, my dear
friend.*
    Henry

Even before Santa folded the letter, Thomas was back telling him
the storm was worsening. That's all Santa needed to hear. He was on his
feet. Buttoning his coat and pulling on his gloves, Santa asked Henry if
he was still up to following him.

"Without a doubt, Santa. I'll be right behind you."

"Steve, I need you to guide us out of here."

"I'll do whatever you ask, Santa."

"I need you to go to the top of this barn and climb out on the roof.
When you feel safe and secure wave the lantern as fast and as high as
you can."

"I'm on my way, Santa."

"I wish you and your family a very merry Christmas, Steve. If you need me, Edmund knows what to do."

"Thank you, Santa. Merry Christmas to you and Mrs. Claus. Have a safe journey."

"Are the sleighs ready, Thomas?"

"Both are ready, Santa. The reindeer are anxious to get going."

"It is time to go, Henry. It will be a rough takeoff. Leave it to the reindeer to get you up and flying."

When Santa boarded his sleigh those colorful crystals were everywhere. Henry followed Santa's lead. Picking up the reins, Santa signaled to his reindeer. Guiding the sleighs out into the field as best he could, Thomas waved them off. It was time for the journey to continue.

"Hold on, Henry. Hold on for the flight of a lifetime!"

The pounding of hoofs against the snowdrifts was deafening even as the wind kept growling. Maybe that was because there were two sleighs, two teams of majestic reindeer pushing their way through the field. They passed trees they could hardly see and hedges buried in white. They forged ahead even faster. Thomas had taught the reindeer well. They knew when to take the leap. They did it simultaneously, performing like a chorus line. Zip! Whiz! Two teams were in the air. Santa caught sight of what he thought was a lantern moving back and forth in the night. The closer he got the more he could tell it was Steve waving with all his might. He inched his way even closer. Henry did the same, holding on tight to the reins. Waiting for the exact moment, Santa let out a yell.

"Steve! Steve! Dancer is ahead of me! Abbey's runt is making the flight once again!"

Watching the lantern move even faster, Santa knew Steve had heard him. Looking around as far as that lantern and the others in trees shed light against the elements, Santa decided to give the sleigh one last test. With a flick of the reins, the reindeer realized what to do. Judging from the sudden force behind him, Santa knew that Henry was still with him.

"Here we go. Here we go," yelled Santa.

With a giant leap ahead, the reindeer soared even higher. Again in sync, they leveled off and just as quickly soared straight down, and then jerked into a complete 360-degree circle so quickly and so smoothly that it was over in an instant. Looking back, Santa caught a glimpse of Henry doing the same. Confident that his sleigh was able to complete the trek, Santa slowed his team and waited for Henry to catch up. When Henry was in sight, Santa gave him the signal. With a nod of his finger and a twinkle in his eye, Santa disappeared into the night. The wind and snow calmed down as the moon took its place on this Christmas Eve.

Henry went for a few more runs. Being a dedicated driver of sleighs, he wasn't ready to call it a night after realizing how back fields had caged him in. Now soaring above the treetops, Henry felt a freedom he'd never experienced. Coming around again, he could make out the farmhouse in the distance. When Henry pulled on the reins, the reindeer reacted, bringing the sleigh down farther. About over the farmhouse, Henry did a quick turnaround, getting even closer. Slowing the team down a bit more, he was level with the upstairs while keeping a lookout ahead. At that moment, he caught sight of Greta standing in the window. They made eye contact. While it was but an instant, Henry knew Greta understood what she saw. Of course he'd tell her she must have been dreaming. After all, it *was* the night of dreams.

Once Henry was back at the barn and the reindeer were bedded down, he made his way to the farmhouse. It wasn't long before he was asleep.

Chapter Thirteen

IT WAS A LITTLE AFTER 11:30 when Meg went back downstairs to check the kids' stockings hanging by the tree. She'd filled them in a hurry. Because the weddings and a house full of company had preoccupied her, she wanted to be sure she hadn't missed anything in her rush to get Christmas ready for Greta and Bobby. It was quiet now. Everyone was sleeping.

While she found she'd placed the right presents in the right stockings and all the presents from Santa were under the tree, Meg realized she hadn't emptied some of the sugar left in a bowl for the reindeer, put any of the milk left for Santa back in the carton, or made it look as if Santa had eaten some of the cookies left out for him. She knew Greta would check, just as Meg had checked when growing up until she was seven. That was the year she'd asked Santa to give her back her family. Since her parents' divorce, Meg never stopped missing being a family. When Santa didn't make that happen, Meg quit believing.

As she was about to open the refrigerator, a sudden brightness coming from outside caught her eye. At first Meg thought it was the moon, now shimmering among the silver stars. But the brightness intensified so that it drew Meg to the back window overlooking fields buried in piles of snow. Meg's attention turned to the barn. It was lit up as she'd never seen it before. She knew Thomas was there. He had to be. Meg put the milk down. Then she went to the back door. With her hand on the knob, she was about to open it. That's when Steve stopped her.

"I was going to see what's happening. Suddenly, the night lit up as if fireworks were going off. It looked more like the 4th of July. It was astonishing!"

"I'd say it's the moon and stars against all that snow. It woke me out of a sound sleep. Once I was awake, I remembered I needed to put a few more things under the tree."

Staying by the door, Meg replied, "I came down to check the stockings."

"It's been a busy few days. You must be exhausted." Steve gently leading Meg further into the kitchen.

"You really think what I saw was the moon and stars?"

"I do. There is so much new snow out there. It's all the perfect combination—and it is Christmas Eve!"

"That means the kids will be up early. Seeing that display outside was the perfect ending to a beautiful day. Good night, Steve. Merry Christmas."

Giving him a hug, Meg went up to bed. Steve waited a few minutes, put his coat and boots on, and walked out the back door. Those crystals were again calling him to the barn. And he knew why.

"Welcome back, Mr. Steve."

"Thank you."

Except for an occasional grunt from the reindeer, the barn was quiet. Thomas led Steve back to that table by the Christmas tree. Edmund was seated in one of the chairs. Thomas and Steve joined him. Hot chocolate had been poured into cups placed in front of them.

"I understand why the crystals fell again, Thomas. I've given consideration to whom I would name to follow me as the reindeer keeper's helper great thought. I realize circumstances may change. I do feel it is important to have this discussion before I relinquish my responsibilities."

Pausing for some hot chocolate, Steve continued. "I thought back to when a stranger chose Abbey's father. That decision stemmed from his daily example of kindness and acceptance to those he knew and to those he didn't. That to me is one deciding factor."

"And keep in mind, young or old, it doesn't matter, Mr. Steve. Santa does not look at age. He looks inside the person."

"I remember you telling me that, as well as the fact it doesn't matter where this person calls home."

"I repeat, that person could be here in a blink of an eye."

"Near or far, young or old, so many factors will be weighed as I make my decision."

Reaching under his chair, Thomas pulled out a small satchel and handed it to Steve. "I made sure Santa brought these letters you asked for with him tonight. He told me to tell you he included the ones he read to Abbey. He has more of Meg's if you feel you need them."

"Thank you, Thomas. I will keep that in mind. I promise to make my decision within the next few days."

The three talked a little longer. Then Steve said good night. On his way out, he felt the urge to go up that narrow stairway again. After checking to make sure Thomas wasn't behind him, Steve went looking for the quick left. Once there, he started up the stairs. Bits of fresh snow were on many of them. Steve's curiosity was heightened as he heard a mumbling—like a whispering—a hushed conversation—coming from the other side of the closed door. He slowly opened it. The light was on. The lantern was still in the window. The trunk was wide open. Greta was sitting on the floor beside it with a book in her lap.

"Grandpa! Hi, Grandpa! What are you doing here?"

Steve was confused. He kept hearing Abbey's voice. His heart quickened. His palms were sweaty. Yes! It was Abbey's voice! He felt dizzy—baffled. His mind was on overload. It was a simple question from a sweet little girl that snapped him into reality.

"Grandpa, are you okay? Want to sit with me and listen to Grandma?"

Staying still, calming down, Steve caught a bit of what he was hearing. It was Abbey, reading *The Night before Christmas*. That was the book Greta was holding. That was what she was listening to.

"Grandma left it for me, Grandpa. She left me a lot of stuff in my trunk."

Now it was making sense. Abbey had recorded the story for the grandchildren she prayed would eventually come.

"I thought you were sleeping. When did you come down here?"

"I couldn't get to sleep so I looked out my window for Santa. And I saw him, Grandpa! He flew right by. He didn't land. I watched. He kept going. That's when I remembered I didn't say good night to Miracle and I wanted Grandma to read me this story again."

Steve couldn't argue the point that it was Christmas Eve and she should be in bed after what she'd said.

"Want to listen to the rest of the story with me, Grandpa?"

"I would love to, Greta."

Climbing into Steve's lap, Greta laughed at some parts and was wide-eyed at others. At the end of the story, Abbey had included a personal message. Steve could tell Greta had heard it more than once. She recited it as Abbey spoke.

> *Merry Christmas my little ones,*
>
> *I hope you enjoyed listening to one of my favorite Christmas stories. I think that's because it is about Santa Claus and his reindeer. Have a happy and a merry Christmas.*
>
> *I love you very much,*
> *Grandma Abbey*

"Your grandmother would have loved holding you, reading to you."

"I know that, Grandpa. She told me."

Steve understood. Abbey's recordings told their grandchildren about believing and Santa and the twinkle in his eye and wonder and everything else a grandmother would tell a grandchild.

"Want to see what else Grandma left me in my trunk?"

"I would love to see what your grandmother left."

While Steve meant what he said, he held back tears not of sadness but of love for a woman who'd brought so much happiness and joy to his life. Sorrow had given way to beautiful memories just as Thomas said it would.

Telling Steve to close his eyes, seconds later, Greta told him to open them.

"Look, Grandpa. Grandma left me a real sketch pad. Daddy said Grandma liked to draw."

Opening his eyes, Steve saw the sketch pad. Not just any sketch pad. He remembered seeing it on the back porch in the winter, near the gardens in the spring and summer, and under trees in the fall. A familiar signature was down in the right hand corner.

"Your daddy is right. Your grandmother loved to draw. She was a very good artist, just like her mother."

"Look at all of Grandma's pictures. She left me some to color."

Going back to the trunk, Greta pulled out another pad. It was smaller. Inside were pages where Abbey had drawn a simple drawing and left room for it to be repeated by little hands she'd never hold.

"See my dinosaur, Grandpa, and my bunny."

"Very good drawings, Greta. Your grandmother would be proud of you."

"I wish I could draw like my grandmother."

"Keep working at it. That's what Grandma Abbey did."

Greta pulled out more items. Steve could tell Abbey had spent hours filling the trunk. Every item had a reason for being included. If she couldn't be here to embrace the first grandchild, every single item would help paint a picture of who she was and how much she loved that child. And from that love, Steve sensed Abbey's hope was the first grandchild would tell her story to any grandchildren following.

"Do you like my mittens? See my doll. Grandma put hair on my doll just like my hair, and she made lots of clothes for her. And look at the blankets, Grandpa. I have a blanket too."

Standing, Greta wrapped a patchwork quilt around her shoulders. She wrapped the smaller quilt around the doll and danced like a ballerina. Then in an instant, she was back, pulling something else from the trunk. Sitting next to Steve and still wrapped in her quilt, Greta took a small diary out of a box.

"Thomas said my grandmother left me a story. When I can't read a word, Thomas helps me. I don't have to ask Thomas very often. It's a good story, Grandpa. You are in it. I like the part where you asked Grandma to dance. She said that made her happy. Was Grandma beautiful with her ponytail? Was she a good dancer like me?"

"Your grandmother was beautiful with her ponytail. She was a good dancer but maybe not quite as good as you."

Sitting on the floor in the top of the barn on Christmas Eve, looking at his granddaughter full of wonder, Steve remembered dancing with Abbey in his arms under the moonlight with snowflakes falling all around.

The two sat there in the quiet. As Steve kept thinking about that dance under the moonlight, another dance came to mind. This dance was more recent. He hadn't planned on anything like that happening. It just did. And now he thought of the woman who'd been his dancing partner quite often.

Who knows how long Steve and Greta would have sat there going through Abbey's diary if it hadn't been for the late hour and Santa's impending visit.

"I think we'd better get going, Greta."

Once down the stairs, Steve took hold of Greta's hand as they headed toward the door. But they never made it. A thundering roar outside the barn came at them from all sides.

Chapter Fourteen

"WHAT IS THAT, GRANDPA?" SCREAMED GRETA, throwing her hands over her ears.

Picking Greta up, Steve turned and hurried farther back in the barn. He didn't know what was going on. Thomas and Edmund came running. It was Thomas who made sense of it all.

"It's the horses, Mr. Steve."

"The horses?"

"The wild horses, Mr. Steve. They've come for Miracle."

Thomas wasn't surprised to find Greta in the barn at such an hour. He knew she often spent time up in what she called her secret spot. And when that time was later in the evening, he'd walk her back to the farmhouse. For some reason her parents never found out. Thomas was certain that was Abbey's doing.

Steve's first instinct was to protect Greta. Losing an animal at any age is hard, but a child losing her pony on Christmas Eve would be heart wrenching.

"Grandpa, I don't want Miracle to leave me."

"I know, Greta. It is very hard to say goodbye to one we love. But I'm sure Miracle's mother would like to bring him home for Christmas."

"But I will miss him," cried Greta.

"Miracle will miss you too, Greta, just like he misses his mommy."

"He misses his mommy? He doesn't look sad. I would be sad if I lost my mommy."

"Ponies don't cry. But that doesn't mean they don't get sad."

Steve now understood the noise. It was hoofs running toward the barn, hoofs digging in the snow. A family had come to bring their little one home. Carrying Greta into the stall and whispering how much he loved her, Steve stopped in front of Miracle's bed of hay. The pony was standing, wagging his tail. He knew who was right outside waiting for him.

"Miracle looks happy, Grandpa."

"That doesn't mean your pony doesn't love you."

"I know," said Greta, wiping away her tears. "I would be happy if my mommy came to get me."

"I'm sure as he grows up, you will see him with the other horses. They are never far away. He will never forget how kind you were to him. He will never forget how much you love him."

"I want to hug Miracle, Grandpa. And then I will take him to his mommy."

Steve was astounded by the maturity Greta was showing. He remembered back when he was young. One week after his father had been killed in Korea, he'd lost his dog. Unconditional love is so hard to lose— just as hard as it is to find.

Putting her down, Steve stepped back. He knew this moment would be one that would stay with Greta throughout her life. When his dog was hit by a car, Steve was the one who found him. He was the one who got a shovel out of the garage and carried his dog around to the back of the house. Steve had been the only one home. His mother was working her second job. His sisters wouldn't have cared even if they had been there.

"Can I take Miracle to his mommy, Grandpa?"

Steve looked to Thomas for advice.

"While wild, that mother will sense the love this child has for her young one, Mr. Steve."

Satisfied with what Thomas said, Steve moved aside as Greta escorted her horse past sacks of grain. The sheep were awake but quiet, as was the cat. Animals can sense what's going on. She didn't wait for Steve to open the door. She gave it one big push. Before stepping outside, Greta gave the little colt a big hug.

"I will miss you, Miracle. But your mommy misses you, too. Everyone needs their mommy."

Greta—with Miracle by her side—stepped in to the night. Steve held back, giving her space, and then followed, as did Thomas and Edmund.

With zillions of glittering stars and magnificent horses pawing the snow, their silky manes moving like whispers in the wind, the moment was spectacular. Once Greta was away from the barn, they inched closer, all together, shaking their manes, snorting, pawing. It didn't scare Greta. She kept moving forward with her pony. Then, all together, the horses stopped. Only one kept moving toward Greta. She was a pinto. Eloquent, proud in stature. Steve heard Greta telling Miracle his mother was beautiful.

"You are so handsome, Miracle," she added.

Hugging him and tenderly stroking his mane, Greta stayed beside her pony. The mother came closer. Miracle ran to her, nudging her over and over. The mother licked her young one's face, pulling the colt close to her while snow fell as gently as the tears of those watching this Christmas Eve story unfold. Greta still didn't move. She looked like a speck against the backdrop of all those magnificent horses. Shaking her head, digging in the snow, the mother nudged toward Greta. Steve was about to make a move but Thomas stopped him.

"She's going to thank Greta, Mr. Steve. She senses the love between the two."

Thomas was right. The mother stood in front of Greta. In winter's beauty, they looked at each other with affection and respect. Greta held a hand out. She spoke softly. "It's okay, Mommy Pinto. No one is going to hurt you."

The mother moved a little closer. She licked Greta's hand. When she put her head down, Greta knew what that meant. Petting her mane and rubbing her forehead, Greta told the mother how much she too loved her pony.

"Take your baby home. It's Christmas."

Looking at each other one last time, the mother turned. So did her pony. As quickly as they came, the horses disappeared into the woods in a tumultuous fury. Snow was rolling up and over the landscape. The thunder of their hoofs slowly drifted away. Greta didn't budge. Picking her up, wiping away her tears, Steve held Greta close all the way home. She went right to bed. Santa was coming.

Chapter Fifteen

DESPITE GETTING TO BED ONLY HOURS earlier, Greta was up shortly after her father made his way down to the kitchen and started to organize breakfast. Eric knew the old house would soon be bustling with excitement. He wanted to get an early start. But once Greta started talking about her pony, he picked her up and hugged her as a flock of chickadees filled the feeders off the back porch.

Eric had so many questions. But listening to Greta tell her story, he realized if he sat and listened those questions would be answered. So, sitting beside her at the kitchen table, he learned about the mommy coming for her colt and why she was at the barn in the first place so late on Christmas Eve.

"I forgot to say good night to Miracle. I knew Thomas was awake. I saw all the lights on. After I hugged Miracle, I . . . I wanted Grandma to read to me."

Greta hesitated. She thought her father might ask what she meant. When he didn't stop her, she explained about the trunk and the recordings and how Thomas would occasionally help her with hard words. By the time Greta explained, Eric couldn't ask a thing. He sat and waited to hear more.

"I like to go there and play, Daddy. Grandma made me a doll with a blanket and mittens and left me her art pad with things to draw. And you were right, Daddy, Grandma loved books. She left me so many. Grandpa sat and listened with me until he thought I should get to bed before Santa Claus came."

By the time Greta got to the part about the wild horses, Meg was standing in the doorway as Christmas morning began with a tender story.

"Thomas knew it was the mommy. All the horses came, Daddy. I told Grandpa I didn't want Miracle to leave me. Grandpa told me Miracle would miss me, just like he missed his mommy. I didn't know Miracle missed his mommy. Then I thought I'd miss my mommy too. And I knew Miracle should be home for Christmas."

Greta paused, looking at Eric. "Everyone should be home for Christmas, Daddy."

Meg joined them, sitting down at the table as Greta explained how she led Miracle outside, told Miracle he was so very handsome, and how the mommy came and licked her hand.

"She put her head down just like Miracle does so I knew she wanted me to pet her. And I did. Then I told her it was time to take her baby home because it was Christmas. So she did, Daddy. The mommy took Miracle back home."

It sounded as if even more chickadees were enjoying themselves as a breeze nudged wind chimes hanging in an old maple in one of the side gardens.

Meg moved next to Greta and held her tight. "I know how Miracle's mommy feels. I would miss my little girl just like she missed her little one. You were a brave little girl, Greta. It isn't easy to say goodbye like you did."

"Grandpa said it is very had to say goodbye to someone you love. I didn't say goodbye to Miracle. Grandpa said I will see him again. He said he would never forget me."

"Grandpa is right. You never forget someone you love," said Eric.

The three sat at the table, talking. As Eric and Meg told their little girl how proud they were of her, Steve came into the kitchen. From the looks on their faces, he knew they were aware of the events that had occurred.

"I could use a cup of coffee."

"It's ready, Dad. From what Greta has told us, you two had quite the time down at the barn."

"That we did, right, honey?" said Steve, giving Greta a wink. "The way that mother horse looked at Greta was something you'd see in a movie."

"Movie? Who's going to the movies?" asked Sammy.

While Steve poured his coffee, he filled Sammy in.

"That's amazing, Greta. I've never heard of a wild horse doing such a thing."

Picking Greta up, Sammy twirled her around the kitchen, wishing her a Merry Christmas. "Something tells me Santa Claus has been here for you and Bobby."

"I know he came, Uncle Sammy. I saw him fly by my window."

"You did?"

As Greta was about to answer, Henry and Sophie walked in.

"I did! Look, Uncle Sammy! Santa is still here."

"Ho! Ho! Ho! Merry Christmas everyone," bellowed Henry. "And a special Merry Christmas to you, Greta."

"Merry Christmas, Santa. Did you see me in the window?"

"I did. You surprised me. I thought you would have been asleep."

"That's a long story," said Steve. "You and Sophie had best get a cup of coffee."

While everyone wished each other a Merry Christmas, Eric went back to cooking. Greta pulled a stool up next to him and asked if she could help.

"I would love a helper," said Eric. "Would you please stir the egg mixture while I check on the jam tats, honey?"

"More jam tarts!" Greta smiled as she whipped eggs in the old cracked bowl.

"Sophie! You have the next generation loving your tarts," said Eric.

"I am honored, Greta. I just heard about your Christmas Eve at the barn my little one. Miracle was lucky to have you as a friend."

"I will be his friend forever. Daddy, can we go to that other barn today?"

"Why do you want to go there?"

"I had a present for Miracle. Thomas said if I brought my present there, Miracle would get it."

"What did you get him?"

"Mommy and I went to the store and bought Miracle a basket of apples and carrots."

"Then I think we should take them there. Maybe we can get Thomas and Henry to drive the sleighs."

"You can count this old Santa in." Henry laughed. "I will need my share of jam tarts to get me going."

"There will be plenty of tarts," said Eric. "My helper and I are making sure of that."

It wasn't long before everyone was up. Cate and Maggie were the last to arrive. Instead of coffee, they poured themselves some juice.

"Good morning, you beautiful brides," said Henry. "Sophie and I were saying yesterday's wedding was the most breathtaking wedding we've ever attended."

"We were saying the same thing, Henry," said Maggie. "We both have friends who've spent thousands of dollars and invested hours in planning and stressing over every little detail. Ironically, we did the opposite, and as you say, it was breathtaking, from the barn, sleighs, snow, and lanterns to the gowns and those gathered. Cate and Sammy—Teddy and I were blessed beyond words."

"It was magnificent," said Cate. "We thank you all for everything you did."

"I'm still replaying it over and over in my mind," said Ellie. "The backdrop with that tree and those bulbs and the sleigh was a treasured Christmas card."

"You won't have to replay yesterday over and over in your mind, Ellie."

"What do you mean, Sammy?"

"With Thomas's help, I had cameras recording the ceremony and celebration. We can watch the video later on this evening."

"I should have guessed my husband the documentarian would do that," said Cate.

"I think watching the video is a fitting end to an amazing gathering."

Everyone agreed. Then the attention turned to Christmas.

Excitement was growing. Eric continued cooking while Meg set the table and Ellie kept her eye on Bobby. Although he didn't grasp the meaning of the day, he did realize there were lots of boxes wrapped in paper that he'd like to tear.

"I remember when Andy was this age. I thought once he was in kindergarten it would get easier. Then I thought the same thing once he was in high school. Truth is it never gets easier. Worrying is the same no matter how old they get."

"I've learned that with Greta. It seems as if she was just born."

"They're always your baby. To think Andy would be in Europe for a Christmas instead of home never crossed my mind as a possibility when he was Bobby's age."

"I'm still digesting the fact Greta was at the barn after midnight surrounded by wild horses, Ellie. Steve and Thomas said she was in no danger but she's so young."

"Young yet wise. It took a certain amount of maturity to take her pony outside to its mother."

"That's why we will be going back to that barn in the woods."

"I heard about the apples and carrots."

"Greta and I made a special trip to the store to buy Miracle a Christmas present. Greta deserves to at least leave it for him."

"I remember when Maggie was three. She had a bunny. We kept it out in the carriage house in the winter. It was plenty warm enough. Christmas Eve she wanted to keep the bunny with her all night. We gave in and Christmas morning we couldn't find the bunny. When we went to open gifts, Maggie found her curled up inside a baby stroller Santa had left by the tree."

"Only goes to prove, Ellie, it's not the baubles you remember."

A knock at the side door interrupted the two.

"Good morning. Merry Christmas," they heard Steve say. "Come in. You are welcome to join us for breakfast."

"Thank you for the invitation, Mr. Steve, but Edmund and I have eaten. We wanted to stop and wish everyone a Merry Christmas and make sure Ms. Greta is okay this morning."

"She's in the kitchen with her father, Thomas. Let me get her."

While Steve went for Greta, Henry happened to walk out of the kitchen.

"Merry Christmas, my friend."

"Merry Christmas, Mr. Henry. It's a marvelous day for sure."

"I was going to find you later to ask if you'd be interested in taking the sleighs into the woods."

Henry explained the reason why.

"Most certainly. Edmund and I will have our duties complete by mid-afternoon. If you like, we could roast marshmallows."

"Marshmallows in the winter?"

"That's when they taste the best, Mr. Henry."

"Where would we be roasting them?"

"When family came last summer, we cleared away an area and built a small outside fireplace behind that barn in the woods. It's perfect for marshmallow roasting. I'll bring along some hot chocolate, some graham crackers, and chocolate bars."

"What a wonderful way to spend Christmas afternoon, Thomas, eating s'mores."

"Indeed, Mr. Henry. And the weather will be clear, mid-twenties."

"Did I hear marshmallows on Christmas?" Steve asked

"You did, Steve."

"Can I have one?" asked Greta.

Thomas explained they would be taking the sleighs into the woods later in the afternoon. Greta would be able to leave Miracle her gift and to make the day even more special, they'd be roasting marshmallows. He also praised Greta for the way she'd handled the horses.

"I miss Miracle. But I know he is happy to be home."

"As I told you, Ms. Greta, he will love your present. Now, Edmund and I have to go. There's much to do, much to do."

Steve and Henry discussed times with Thomas out on the back porch while Eric finished the omelets and pulled coffee cakes and quiche out of the oven. The French toast was being kept warm, as were the scrambled eggs and sausages, and of course, the jam tarts. He'd made more coffee. Ellie filled glasses with freshly squeezed orange juice while Meg lit the candles—then put Bobby in his high chair. Everything was ready. Of course Greta would have preferred to be opening gifts, especially the one big one with her name on it.

Once everyone was gathered around the table, Steve said the blessing. There was much to be thankful for this Christmas morning. Dishes were passed. Conversation flowed. A phone ringing in the kitchen caught Sammy's attention.

"I'll get it."

He was back in a second.

"Dad it's for you. She said her name was Susan."

"Excuse me," said Steve, his face a little red, "I'll just be a minute."

When he returned, Greta was the first to speak.

"Grandpa! I have a friend named Susan!"

"I know you do. I met her one day at your school."

"Can I meet your friend, Grandpa?"

"Maybe. We'll see. She's an old friend of mine. I ran into her at my class reunion this past summer."

Sammy asked if she lived nearby.

"About twenty miles down Route 93. After Christmas, she'll be going to Maine for the winter."

"Not Florida?"

"No, Cate. Susan is like Abbey and I used to be. She has no interest in Florida. She and her husband had a home near Portland. After he passed away a few years back, Susan decided to keep it. She's an artist. She has a studio there."

"An artist like Mom?"

"Yes, Eric, an artist like your mother."

"I think it's nice you've reconnected with an old friend, Dad. I'm sure we drive you silly sometimes."

"You've never mentioned Susan." While Meg seemed surprised, her smile showed how happy she was for him.

Refilling his cup, Steve asked Henry to pass the sugar. Once he added a dash or two, Steve stirred the coffee in the china cup he'd bought

Abbey on their tenth anniversary. Putting the spoon down and biting his bottom lip like he always did when he'd get nervous, Steve talked about that old friend as the candles flickered.

"To be honest, Meg, I didn't know how to."

No one spoke so Steve kept talking.

"I enjoy her company. We happened to meet again after years had passed us by."

"When I look around this table," said Sophie, "I see young love and old love and rekindled love. I see a parent's love and that of a child. Love is defined by the heart. And every heart has its own rhythm of time."

"Thanks, Sophie. I understand what you are saying."

"I'm happy for you, Dad. Mom would be too," said Sammy.

"Invite her to dinner. We'd love to meet her."

"Thank you, Eric. I've thought about that, but it felt awkward. Enough talk, let's enjoy this wonderful meal and get to those presents."

"One more thing, Dad. I think you should plan a trip to Maine this winter."

"We'll see. That feels awkward, too, Sammy."

Steve could tell by his sons' expressions they were trying to accept the thought of his being in the company of another woman. Moving on can sometimes prove more challenging than ever imagined.

Chapter Sixteen

To Greta's delight, it wasn't long before they were in the front room. Presents were everywhere. Steve stoked the fire while Ellie made sure Sophie and Henry were comfortable on the sofa. Meg handed Eric Bobby's stocking. The little one was more interested in the bells hanging from strings of yarn.

"That's always the way," said Ellie. "You buy expensive toys and it's some inexpensive little thing that catches their eye. Remember the year Andy was obsessed with my new coffee pot, Ben?"

"How could I forget that? I stayed up half the night putting a Big Wheel together and he went for the coffee pot."

"We all have those stories," said Steve. "I can recall one year when Abbey and I couldn't wait for the boys to come down and find new sleds under the tree. But plastic bats and balls from Abbey's brother grabbed their attention instead. They played baseball out in the snow most of the day."

"Moral of the story, Meg and I shouldn't have worried whether or not we'd get it right come Christmas morning."

"That's the gist of it, Eric."

Greta was so excited. Paper was flying off little gifts stuffed inside the knit stocking with reindeer in flight. Bobby tried catching the paper.

He had no interest in what was inside his stocking so Eric dug in and helped him. Meg handed out the gifts piled under the tree. When she put a certain one in Sammy's lap, Cate was all smiles.

"I don't even have to read the tag. I can tell this is from my beautiful bride."

Ripping away the paper, Sammy opened a plain white box. The look of surprise written all over his face said Cate had nailed it.

"Where did you find this?"

"The night we met on that train heading to Barcelona, you wrote your address inside a small notepad and handed it to me as we rushed off in different directions. That was inside. I never knew it was there until a few months ago."

"I wondered where it went."

"You know how I believe things happen for reasons. I think I was meant to find this."

"There's nothing you could have given me that would have meant more to me."

Turning the frame around for everyone to see, Sammy explained the significance of what was written on a sheet of paper.

"The night Cate sat down next to me on that train, I was working on this. I fell for her the minute we started talking. That's when I shoved this inside the notepad. When it was time to go our separate ways, I scribbled my information inside the notepad and handed it to her, forgetting this was in there."

"What is it?"

"It's a rough sketch of my logo, Dad, with the first draft of my mission statement scribbled underneath."

"I agree with Cate. Things happen for reasons. That might be all you need to get your juices flowing again."

"I'm after a story no one else would notice. A story that's simple yet moving."

"Mommy, Daddy! Look what Santa brought me! New cowgirl boots and a hat and some chaps and a snowsuit! And they're all pink!"

Running over to Henry, Greta threw her arms around him.

"Thank you, Santa. This is what I wanted!"

The wonder of a child believing filled Henry's heart. Being Santa came with perks. In a whisper he told Greta she was welcome.

"I wish Miracle could see what you gave me, Santa."

"Maybe he will. I'm sure he's not far away."

They kept unwrapping surprises. Ben's gift to Ellie of tickets to the opening of a Broadway show was unexpected since she'd been told they were sold out. Henry's gift of handwritten poetry in a simple binder brought Sophie to tears.

"You two are quite the romantics. I'm afraid I went for the practical," said Sammy as Meg handed Cate his present.

Within seconds the photographer uncovered what had been at the top of her list although she never said a word to anyone about it.

"Oh, Sammy. How did you know? This is the Canon I've looked at over and over!"

"Call it instinct. You deserve to have the best camera made to show the world what I already know about your talent."

"I'll try it out later when we're in the sleigh. I read it adapts instantly to speed. Thank you, my love."

Teddy surprised Maggie with a stunning silver watch, explaining the watch represented the commitment they'd made through good times and bad.

"You are as much a romantic as Henry," said Ellie.

"It's a beautiful gift, Teddy. I love it."

Bobby found interest in a small wooden train. Greta kept unwrapping presents. Eric was enthralled with old cookbooks that had been his mother's.

"I've never seen these before, Meg. Look. Mom made notes along the side of some of the recipes. I bet they were her favorites. I do the same thing."

"I was in the attic looking for picture frames when I came across them."

Steve explained Abbey bought the cookbooks when they were newlyweds living in Charleston.

As Meg handed out the last few gifts, Eric walked out of the room. He returned carrying an oversized box.

Eric told Meg the gift was for her.

"But I only gave you your mother's cookbooks and didn't spend a penny."

"Those cookbooks are priceless, honey. It's not what you spend. It's more about the thought behind the gift."

Meg lifted the bag off what turned out to be a computer.

"Eric! You shouldn't have. The computer I have is fine."

"You deserve the best, Meg. I don't know how you do all that you do."

The room was buried in paper. Coffee cups were refilled and gifts examined as piano classics played.

"What a beautiful Christmas," said Sophie. "Yesterday, today—both so magical."

"We have one sleigh ride to go," said Henry. "Thomas will be here around two o'clock."

"That gives the boys and I time to go to the cemetery."

"The cemetery, Steve?" asked Henry.

"It's a tradition Abbey started, taking us to visit her parents' grave site."

"I remember now. You talked about that in your documentary."

"I did. Mom taking us to the cemetery on Christmas was the catalyst, Henry. Now we go back every Christmas."

"I can't remember if my family had traditions. I don't remember much about them," said Sophie.

"We'll start our own traditions. And we will pass them down."

"I'd love to do that, Henry."

"You already have, Mom."

"How so, Benny?"

"With your jam tarts!"

Everyone agreed. Sophie's jam tarts would be a tradition.

While Greta and Bobby played, plans were made for later on. Excitement had only heightened on this the most wondrous day of the year.

Chapter Seventeen

Due to a problem with the back door of the barn not shutting, Thomas was running behind schedule. It worked out for the best since Steve and the boys were late getting back from the cemetery.

"I didn't give much thought as to how much snow there'd be. Some drifts were impassable," said Steve, when Meg asked about their visit.

"Any time I've gone with you, there's always been a lot of snow. The plows never bother to go too far in on Christmas."

"Plows never even made an attempt this year," said Eric. "Funny thing, though, around mom's gravesite, the wind seemed to have cleared much of the snow away. Rabbit tracks were everywhere."

"I'm not surprised, honey," smiled Meg.

Minutes later Eric started dinner while Henry went down to the barn. When they were off in the woods, some of his staff would be coming in and finishing the full-course meal. Eric wanted it to be a memorable experience on their last night together. There'd be an extra place setting at the table.

Sleigh bells soon announced Thomas and Henry's arrival. Edmund stayed behind to finish feeding the reindeer. Everyone knew where to sit from the sleigh ride the day before. Once Sophie was situated, they were ready to go. The apples and carrots were at Greta's feet. This time, Bobby was going along.

"It's a beautiful winter's day to break in my new camera."

"I wouldn't know how to even turn one of those on." Sophie laughed.

"They only look complicated," said Sammy.

"I used to think my Brownie camera was difficult."

"Anything new seems that way. For someone like Cate, she has the eye for it," said Ben.

"I've seen some of your photos, young lady. You are quite talented."

"Thanks, Sophie. Hopefully today will generate some great opportunities."

After checking to make sure everyone was tucked in tight, Thomas nodded to Henry and off they went again. If anyone could have ordered perfect weather, this day would have been the result. Tree branches and hedges were dusted with snow. With the sun filtering through, they glittered against the clear blue sky. No one spoke. There was too much to take in. The horses knew where they were headed. Thomas had made the trip earlier to get a fire going. Any evidence of that trip was about covered up by the slight wind still blowing. Despite the snow being so heavy in some places, they forged ahead—silver bells ringing out across the fields.

Once near the woods, Thomas and Henry slowed them down. Maneuvering about the trees was as tricky as before yet the horses pranced their way around each one. It wasn't long before the lanterns could be seen in the distance. That's all Cate needed.

"Thomas! Could we stop for a minute once we get a little closer?"

Thomas didn't say a word. Rather he waved his hand over his head—then pulled the sleigh to a halt. Henry did the same.

"Will this do, Miss Cate?"

"Perfect. Thank you. I will only take a second."

Jumping off the sleigh, Cate was buried in snow. But it didn't stop her. After getting her bearings, Cate situated herself not far from the others and took some shots. On the way back to the sleigh, she took a few more of the smiling faces watching her.

Minutes later, the horses pulled the sleighs behind that other barn, stopping near a side door. The path Thomas had shoveled was still passable. Ben and Steve helped Sophie into the barn.

"Come with me, Greta. We'll put your apples and carrots out for

Miracle. Don't be sad if he doesn't show up while we are here. He might wait until dark."

"Will he come by himself, Daddy?"

"No. Thomas said his mother and all the wild horses will come since they are a family."

"I don't have enough apples and carrots for all the horses."

"They won't care. They'll all be protecting Miracle."

"That's a nice family, Daddy."

"It is a nice family, Greta."

Eric and Greta put the carrots and apples more out in the open than under trees in an area Thomas had cleared earlier. That way there'd be room for all the horses to circle Miracle. On their way into the barn, Eric told his little girl how pretty she looked in her pink snowsuit.

"Look! It has a pony on it, Daddy".

"I see the pony, honey. It looks like Miracle."

Thomas and Meg had found small branches for the marshmallows and started a fire in the outside fireplace. While waiting for the fire to die down, everyone sat on the benches near the tree with all the shiny glass ornaments and sipped on hot chocolate. Bobby lasted for about five minutes. Those ornaments caught his eye. When Meg walked with him down the steps to the tree, Greta followed. It only took her a second to notice a change.

"Look, Santa. Your bag fell off the seat of your sleigh. It's open. It looks like something is still in there."

Greta was trying to climb on board. Henry was there to stop her.

"I'll get the bag, Greta. I must have dropped it last night."

Reaching inside the old sleigh, Henry grabbed hold of the bag. Thanks to Thomas, Henry realized its history. Knowing it was that other Santa's original satchel was a bit powerful. The leather was soft. The strap was worn, and to his surprise, there really was something inside. Henry took his time opening it more than it already was. He sensed Thomas watching his every move. Once he pulled the front flap back the rest of the way, Henry pulled the sides out and reached inside. His fingers felt something. Making sure he had a good hold of whatever it was, Henry pulled, and then he pulled a little harder.

The sun coming through the stained glass sent colors swirling about the old barn as Henry held on to an old box shaped like a heart. It seemed to have once been a rich velvet material, but years had turned it worn and tattered. A tarnished gold clasp was still keeping the box shut. As he was about to place it on a nearby table, a loud gasp echoed up to the rafters and back. Turning, Henry saw Sophie standing, crying. Ben was beside her.

"What is it, Mom? Are you sick?"

Sophie kept crying and pointing at Henry.

"Mom? Mom!"

Ben was almost yelling at her. Fear does that when you fear the worst.

"Henry! Henry," she sobbed. "Henry!

"What, Sophie? We can leave right now."

"Henry! That box. I remember that box being in my parents' bedroom. It sat on a dresser covered with a starched doily. It was an antique dresser—a mahogany antique highboy dresser with two small drawers at the top and four bigger ones below. I remember going into the bedroom when no one was around. I'd take the box off the dresser. Then I'd sit down on the bed—covered in a matelassé bedspread that matched the one on my father's bed—open it, and look at all my mother's favorite things—from a string of pearls she'd worn on her wedding day to an antique cameo broach she'd wear every Christmas Eve with matching earrings and ring. I loved the ring. I'd wear it as I sat there looking at all those beautiful pieces of jewelry. My favorite was never kept in the box. It was a silver locket. Inside the locket was a picture. It was of Lily and me. My mother wore it every day. I remember Henry! I remember my parents' twin beds with a small nightstand between them. The walls were covered in printed wallpaper. The colors were soft against the varnished window casings. I remember, Henry! I remember."

Handing the box to Ben, Henry embraced his Sophie.

"My love, I don't understand this. I believe you, but I don't understand."

Thomas stepped forward. If anyone could make sense of what was going on, it was Thomas.

"Miss Sophie, some moments are unexplainable. Forces work in ways we will never understand but if your heart and mind are in the right place, whatever is being worked on, whatever is being dealt with, or whatever is coming together will occur and be understood by those willing to put their faith on the line when nothing makes sense."

Wiping her eyes and taking a deep breath, Sophie spoke. "So much that I shoved out of my mind has come back to me in the last few minutes. I remember that little girl inside me. I remember my mother braiding my hair in the early morning while the oatmeal was cooking. I can smell the iron heating up and hear my sister cry when it was her turn to get her hair braided. I can vaguely see my father—tall with a mustache—dressed in a tweed suit and smelling of pipe tobacco. My mother—my mother—so beautiful, with gentle eyes and delicate hands. Whatever is going on at this moment, I pray it will continue. I believe a force greater than I could ever understand put that box in that satchel to be found at this moment. I am filled with joy, Thomas."

"You must keep in mind, Miss Sophie the resolution is sometimes not what we wish."

"But at least one would have the answer and with that comes peace."

"I could not have expressed it any better, Miss Sophie."

"May I hold the box?"

"I believe that is the plan, Miss Sophie. In fact, I believe you are to take the box home with you."

"Oh my! That would go beyond my expectations, Thomas."

"I don't think that is true from what I have heard."

"What do you mean?"

"I and others are aware of your kindness and generosity. A person without expectations is a person narrow in character. That is not you, Miss Sophie."

Ben agreed as he extended the worn blue box to his mother. Henry sat next to Sophie as she pulled up on the tarnished gold clasp and discovered old yellowed photos of a family long since torn apart. Sometimes families allow things to happen without realizing what they are giving up. Once they do, often the harm done stands in the way of healing.

Except for Meg who was busy with Bobby, everyone sat quietly in the benches of that old barn while Sophie looked at faces she'd blocked from her mind and heart. But it was something underneath all those photos that had her shaking—had tears flowing down her cheeks.

"Oh my," she whispered.

"What is it?" Henry asked.

Grabbing hold of the object, Sophie explained "It's the locket! It's my mother's locket, Henry."

Sunlight continuing to filter through stained glass windows created a spectrum of colors—a winter rainbow swirling about as Sophie pulled the locket out of its resting place for what probably had been years upon years and held it in her hands—rubbing away dust and a few bits of tissue paper it'd been half-wrapped in. Although tarnished, the locket's intricate design was apparent.

"My heart is aching, Henry. I am an old woman missing my mother."

"Age does not matter. You're always a child when thinking of your mother. I do the same. I loved bringing wood in from the shed. Most often my mother would be standing by the wood stove cooking. She'd smile the warmest smile every time I stacked the wood."

"I see my mother sitting in the parlor by the oval window overlooking her perennials. She's knitting. I can smell lavender, Henry. She'd knit sachets to hold the scent of lavender in dresser drawers. Lily and I would sit on the floor and play with the toy train set our father brought back from one of his business trips while Mama knitted."

A look of astonishment came over Sophie's face.

"What is wrong? Is this all too much?"

Staring at the locket, Sophie wept. It took her a few minutes.

"Did you hear what I said, Henry?"

"About the train?"

"No. No. I called my mother Mama. I called her Mama when we lived in that home as a family and everyone was happy and safe and . . . ."

Sophie stopped. "Oh my, Henry! I never realized until now how I take after my mother. I use my hands to create as she did. My needle and thread are my instruments as knitting needles were her's."

With Bobby getting restless, Sophie opened the locket. But only for a moment. While overwhelmed, she felt the moment was a private one to be cherished with Henry once they were back in their old stone home. So she closed the locket, put it back underneath the yellowed photos, shut the box and suggested they roast marshmallows.

Chapter Eighteen

"THE COALS FROM THE FIRE SHOULD be ready," said Thomas.

Greta jumped to her feet. Of course Bobby had never stopped. Making sure her coat was zipped and her scarf and hat were snug, Eric took Greta's hand. It was still a sight to behold—all those trees dressed in snow with the sun sifting through. They went to see if Miracle's gifts had been eaten.

"There still here, Daddy. Maybe Miracle doesn't like my present."

"I've never heard of a horse not liking carrots and apples. We'll come back later."

That worn old box had caused quite a stir. Everyone was out behind the barn, taking turns hugging Sophie and adding their good wishes and amazement at what had been found. Being the one who pieced things together to make a story, Sammy wanted to do the same with what had taken place but Sophie reminded him there was no logic to that box being there.

"Logic isn't a part of this conversation. While we search for reasons, sometimes there are none that make sense. I believe that box was meant to be found at that very moment. The rest of it is out of my hands."

"I respect what you are saying. I've come across a few instances like that. But this is the most astonishing."

"I told you—my Sophie is amazing, Sammy!"

"You did, Henry, and you were right."

"Time for winter marshmallows," said Steve. "There should be enough sticks. If you want to turn your marshmallow into a s'more, graham crackers and chocolate bars are over there on that cart."

Cate had her camera ready as they roasted marshmallows and shared conversation. Bobby preferred eating them right out of the bag. Just as the last of the s'mores were made, a dull sound like distant thunder could be heard. No one thought too much of it until that dull sound became more of a roar and the earth seemed to shake.

"It's the horses," said Thomas. "The wild horses are coming!"

Taking hold of Greta, Eric walked behind Steve and Thomas. Meg held Bobby close and followed. With creative juices flowing, Sammy ran for his video camera. Because the snow was so deep, Henry led Sophie back through the barn and out another door.

With trees blocking the horizon the only inkling of what was approaching was that roar getting louder. Bobby cried, nuzzling closer to his mother. This time, Greta was not afraid. She didn't put her hands over her ears. She stood waiting for Miracle.

The closer the horses came, the more the snow flew about like a blinding snowstorm in the midst of calm and blue skies. Sammy was capturing it all. Cate was taking frame after frame. In the heart of the fury, silhouettes of galloping horses were emerging. Powerful, majestic—the horses kept coming, their manes flying, their hoofs breaking through the drifts. Winter birds disappeared. Rabbits hid. Greta stood her ground, waiting for the pony she'd nursed back to health and fell in love with along the way.

The wall of horses came to a halt near the old barn. When the lead stallion made the first move, Greta remained vigilant. As he made his way to the carrots and apples, the lead mare followed. They didn't eat but instead sniffed around and then turned and approached Greta. Sammy inched closer as she extended her hand. It was a powerful moment, with the snow swirling and the other horses stomping their hoofs, churning the white stuff all about. Those mighty steeds stood still as the little girl patted them, telling them how beautiful they were and how happy she was that Miracle was with them. Then she walked toward the carrots and apples. The two horses followed. Both Cate and Sammy struggled to contain themselves. Picking up an apple in one hand and a carrot in the other, Greta turned and offered the gifts to the two behind her.

Sammy zoomed in on Greta's hand holding the apple and the mighty stallion bending over to accept it. The stallion and Greta met eye to eye. Cate snapped that brief second as well, breaking it down into millionths of a second to catch the blinking of their eyes, the steam rolling out of the stallion's nose, and the tears in Greta's eyes. Then in one swift move, the apple disappeared without Greta's pink mitten ever being touched. The attention turned to the mare sniffing the carrot. As she nodded her head, the carrot disappeared as well. Greta offered them a few more.

"Go ahead. Take them."

And so they did. As they were leaving, the horses stopped in front of Greta.

"Merry Christmas. I am so happy you came."

"My God, Sammy. This is out of the ballpark."

"It's not over yet. Here comes Miracle."

The band of horses moved in a little closer and then stopped. Walking out from their midst came Miracle. His mother followed.

"Get ready, Cate. Here comes the heartbreaker."

Falling on her knees—just about getting buried in the snow—Greta held out her arms as she called to her pony.

"It's me, Miracle! It's me!"

The colt leapt over the snow, landing inches from Greta. Scooping Miracle up in her arms, Greta kept telling Miracle how much she missed him. After a few minutes, Greta got to her feet.

"Come see what I brought you."

As they approached the apples and carrots, Miracle started prancing.

"I love when you do that, Miracle. That means you're happy! So am I."

Once Miracle spotted what was waiting for him, he made a dash to the closest apple.

"You're so cute, Miracle. Eat as many as you want. I'm going to give a few to your mother."

Both Sammy and Cate moved closer.

"These are for you, Mommy Horse."

Extending her hand, Greta waited. The horse didn't budge.

"Don't be afraid. I am your friend."

Greta kept her hand extended as she walked toward the mother.

Sammy zoomed in on Greta's face.

"Here," said Greta. "These are for you."

Shaking her head up and down while pawing the snow, the mother looked first at her colt and then Greta. She kept it up. Greta didn't wait. She walked in front of the horse and lifted her hands up as far as she could. The mother devoured the carrot and then the apple.

"Here's one more."

Greta reached in her pocket and offered the mother the apple. It was gone in a jiffy. The black stallion became restless, signaling it was time to leave. Greta sensed she had to say goodbye.

"I will see you soon, Miracle. I'll bring you more to eat."

Hugging her little friend and then patting the mother, Greta stepped aside. Once the mother turned around and went back to the horses, Miracle did the same. The stallion shook his head, turned, and galloped away. All the other horses followed.

Just as Sammy and Cate were about to take a breath, Thomas came around from behind the barn in a sleigh ready to go. In the back were Henry and Steve.

"Jump in. You can film as we follow the band."

Without hesitating, Sammy and Cate reacted. They were about to jump in when Greta came running.

"I want to go, too!"

There was no time to argue. Sammy picked her up and climbed into the sleigh. Off they went. Sammy started filming as soon as he zeroed in on the cloud of snow ahead. Thomas let his team go. Once out of the woods, they were soaring alongside the wild horses. Sammy and Cate caught it all—their might—their beauty—their hoofs digging in, determined to stay free. Glimpses of Miracle running alongside his mother came and went with the wind. Realizing what lay ahead, Thomas pulled back on the reins. The band never faltered. Jumping over a fence, they disappeared in that cloud of snow. The sleigh came to a stop.

"That was unbelievable," said Sammy. "I could have touched a few of them. Amazing—a band of wild horses right out the back door."

"I saw Miracle looking at me."

"I did too," said Cate. "I took his picture. I even think he was smiling at you."

"Miracle has a nice smile."

"Thomas, you are a master of the sleigh. I commend you."

"That is a compliment indeed, Mr. Henry, coming from a master such as you."

"I can't wait to see what we have, Sammy."

"I am thinking the same thing, honey. What a way to spend a honeymoon!"

"I wouldn't want to be anywhere else."

Thomas took it slow getting back to the others. What they'd experienced needed to be savored.

Chapter Nineteen

EVEN THOUGH IT WAS DARK WHEN returning to the farmhouse, those lanterns in the trees led them out of the woods. Then the stars and moon took over. Nestled under blankets and in his mother's arms, Bobby fell sound asleep. Greta found comfort nuzzled next to Sophie. It was a little before six by the time they made it home. When the sleighs came to a stop, everyone knew the routine. Even before they made it through the back door, delicious aromas coming from the kitchen filled their senses.

"I didn't think I was hungry," said Teddy. "But I was wrong."

"Eric has a special menu for our last night together," said Meg.

With their snowsuits off, Greta and Bobby ran to play with new toys waiting for them under the tree. Steve built the fire in the fireplace. After ensuring everything was in place, Eric helped Meg carry those long-stemmed glasses on silver trays into the front room. Once filled with whatever preferred, Steve proposed a toast. But a knock at the back door interrupted him. Steve hurried to answer it.

"It must be Thomas," said Ben. "Dad asked me to set another place at the table."

But it wasn't Thomas. Instead, it was a woman—a tall, slender woman with hair the color of mahogany falling just past her shoulders. Except for green eyes enhanced by a bit of eyeliner, she wore no makeup.

There was no need. With her arm in Steve's, the woman made her entrance into the front room.

Eric could tell his father was apprehensive so he hurried over to ease his nerves. As he did, images of his mother filled Eric's mind and heart. He knew she was smiling down on them. Life goes on, Abbey would tell her boys. She learned that at an early age living above her father's funeral home.

"You must be Susan. I'm Eric, the oldest son. I'd like to welcome you to our home. This is my wife, Meg. Under the tree, playing, are Greta and Bobby, our children."

"It's a pleasure to meet you both. Your father has told me so much about all of you."

"I'm the favorite son," said Sammy, extending his hand to a woman he sensed he'd be seeing more of as time went on. Memories of Abbey flooded Sammy's heart as well. For some reason while shaking this woman's hand, thoughts of his first sleepover came to mind. Abbey had packed his favorite pajamas and favorite blanket. Sammy insisted he was a big boy. He didn't need his blanket. In the middle of the night, he woke up. He wanted to go home. Grabbing hold of that blanket, he rolled over and went back to sleep after crying into his pillow so his friend just a few feet away wouldn't hear him. When morning came, Sammy called his mother first thing. She was there in an instant. When he shut the car door, Abbey told her little boy how much she'd missed him.

"I missed you too, Mommy."

Now, grown up and married, Sammy missed her even more as his father introduced his friend Susan to everyone in the room with a tree reaching about to the ceiling. While Steve made small talk, Sammy's thoughts went to the angel sitting on the highest branch.

Cate knew he was thinking about the daughter his parents had lost at birth, a sister Sammy never knew. Taking his hand, Cate walked over to the tree. She felt he needed to talk but not everyone needed to hear.

"Mom would always say she was our angel in heaven watching over us, Cate. I feel her presence tonight."

"Sisters have a way of taking care of brothers, honey. Please realize you're not abandoning your mother if you get to know Susan. Your mother taught you about life and death through her words and deeds. She prepared you for this day. She prepared all of us."

"I love you, Cate. You can read me like a book."

"I'm right beside you, my love. Everything is going to be fine."

Joining the others, Sammy eased his way into the conversation. Susan made it effortless.

"I've watched your documentaries. You have a gift in the way you get to the core of a story without preaching. You lead the viewer there without the viewer realizing it."

"Thanks, Susan. That's the power of a documentary. The voice a documentary provides simply tells a story whatever that story might be, from injustice to wild horses."

As soon as he said it, Sammy looked at Cate. The light bulb had gone off.

"That's it, Cate! That's the next story to be told."

"It is! You wanted a story no one else would notice, a moving story unlike anything you've done before."

"Thanks again, Susan. You made me realize the story I've been searching for is right in front of me."

"I don't know what I did but I'm happy to have helped. It drives me nuts when I look at a blank canvas and I'm void of any inspiration or idea of what to paint. It's a frightening experience."

"It's a place I try to avoid but that doesn't always happen. Dad told us you are an artist."

"I hope your father explained I'm a struggling artist."

"I don't know an artist who doesn't struggle in some way. For me I'm never happy with the result. I watch a finished film and wish I'd used a different angle or shot a scene in black and white instead of color. I am my own worst critic."

"I do the same. I'm never happy, never quite sure if I'm finished with a piece."

"Abbey did the same, Susan. I don't remember her ever liking anything she painted," said Steve.

"On occasion I remind myself painting beats being tied to a desk from eight to five," said Susan. "The freedom is worth the anguish we put ourselves through."

"I agree. And now that I know what my next project is, the ideas are coming one right after another."

"Does that mean our daughter is going to Hollywood?" asked Meg.

"That means Greta and Miracle will be friends forever on film. The Hollywood part I will leave to others to decide."

Conversation continued in that old farmhouse. It wasn't long before dinner was ready.

"I enjoy your restaurant, Eric," said Susan as she and Steve walked into the dining room. "Your asparagus chicken is a favorite of mine."

"I appreciate your business. Since I spend most of my time in the kitchen, I can't say I remember seeing you in the dining room."

"Even if you weren't in the kitchen, you probably wouldn't have seen me. I do takeout most of the time, especially if I'm working on a painting."

"I can't stop when I'm sewing one of my snowmen until I'm done."

"Steve told me about your snowmen and the beautiful story behind them."

"Life is a continuing story, Susan. The longer you live, the more chapters you get to write."

Once Greta and Bobby were in place, the others sat down at the table. Steve was at the head. Next to him sat Susan. It felt odd for those who'd gathered around that table for Christmas dinner in years past. When Eric placed the platter holding the prime rib in front of his father, it became awkward. It was the same platter used for as long as anyone could remember. Henry sensed what was happening.

"This reminds me of Christmas growing up on the farm. My father always did the carving. My mother always did the running around. After my father passed away, it wasn't the same, but after a while, a new tradition replaced the old. That's how it goes, you know. Traditions change as families change."

That's all it took for the roast to be carved and dishes brought out from the kitchen and passed from one to another. Praises were given to

Eric and his staff. When it was time for dessert, out came a tray with three choices. Everyone had a hard time choosing.

"That's the most beautiful yule log I've ever seen," said Ellie.

"Food should be pleasing to the eye. Sitting down to a meal should arouse all our senses. Unfortunately, most of the time, we are in too much of a hurry."

"That's what I love about the French and Italians," said Susan. "The meal is a celebration."

"My heritage is French-Canadian. Henry kids me it's the reason my pea soup is so delicious."

"I've read studies on that," said Eric. "Growing up, we acquire a taste for a mainstay served in the home. That follows us as we become adults and we're the ones preparing the meals. We have a barometer to go by."

"Cooking has become a valued commodity. You'd make quite the handsome TV chef, Eric."

"Thanks, Sophie, but I prefer to put my time and efforts into the restaurant. It's all I've ever wanted. I've watched others expand into television. To me, most of them are one generic brand. I prefer to stay true to who I am as a chef."

"Expansion can do that if you're not careful. It can also do you in," said Steve.

"I know my waistline is expanding after this phenomenal meal," joked Henry.

Everyone shared a laugh as desserts were savored. Once everyone finished, after-dinner liqueurs were enjoyed in the front room while Eric's staff went to work on cleaning up.

"What time are you airing the wedding video, Sammy?"

"Whenever you are able to sit down Meg."

"All I have to do is get the kids bathed and in their pajamas."

"I'm afraid I must be going," said Susan. "I want to thank everyone for welcoming me into your home. I know it wasn't easy. I understand. I've had a lovely evening, but I'm leaving for Maine within the week and haven't done a thing to get ready."

Goodbyes were exchanged as Steve went for Susan's coat.

"I'll be interested to hear how that documentary is going, Sammy."

"I'll keep Dad updated."

A LITTLE OVER AN HOUR LATER the front room was in darkness except for the tree lights and the fire crackling. Just as Sammy was ready to get the show underway, Eric walked in with bowls of popcorn. While everyone insisted they were full, the bowls were refilled a few times as the day before unfolded in front of them.

As the last few minutes were playing, Sammy promised everyone a copy of the video. Bobby and Greta never heard a word. They were sound asleep.

"We better follow the little ones' example," said Sophie. "Tomorrow will be a long journey back home."

"It will be if this snow keeps up," said Ben, looking out toward the barn.

"It could all change by morning. I've seen it happen countless times," said Eric.

"We can always go by sleigh," added Henry.

They said their good-nights.

Chapter Twenty

THE PLAN WAS FOR BEN, ELLIE and family to be on the road by nine if the weather was good. Turned out the weather was not the problem. It all happened so fast.

With breakfast over, Henry was on his way to spend a few minutes with Thomas before leaving. The thunder of hoofs pounding the earth stopped him midway. Looking toward the woods, Henry waited. Thomas and Edmund heard the rumble. They came outside and waited as well. While in the house playing, Greta heard the thunder. Everyone was off the back steps in an instant. Sammy and Cate grabbed their cameras.

The mighty stallion was first to appear. Standing at the edge of the trees, he hesitated. Once joined by the lead mare and others in the band, he proceeded as snow swirled up and around with their every movement. Greta sensed something had happened. Without a word, she walked through the drifts to meet the stallion. Despite his power and might, the stallion dropped his head and nuzzled in Greta's arms. Licking her head and cheeks, he stayed put. The mare followed, taking her turn to be embraced by the little girl in a pink cowgirl snowsuit. A few minutes later, the rest of the band circled Greta. In the middle of those wild horses was Miracle's mother. But there was no Miracle. Greta searched for her pony. She waited for Miracle to come leaping toward her, but that didn't happen. The longer they stood there, the more compassion those lead horses gave to the little one who'd cared for one of their own with a love that was obvious even to horses deemed wild and free.

"My Miracle is gone, isn't he?" Greta asked the stallion. "You came to tell me Miracle is gone."

The stallion moved even closer, as did the mare. Keeping her distance, Miracle's mom seemed at a loss. Greta sensed her sorrow and realized any mother of any child would be overwhelmed with grief. Walking among the horses, Greta didn't hesitate to reach up as far as she could to hold that mother.

"I loved Miracle too. I will miss him, Mommy Horse. I know how much he loved you. I saw it in his eyes. A mommy's love is a special love."

Meg broke down when hearing her daughter's words. At that moment, Meg forgave her mother. She let go of resentments held for years. She accepted what Abbey had said about Meg not having walked in her mother's shoes. She accepted the fact that her mother had done the best she could. Standing in the drifts watching her own daughter, Meg understood the deeper meaning of being a mother. She felt the pain of the mother horse. She felt the need to embrace her mother. Meg prayed it was not too late.

With the wind shifting, the lead stallion became restless. Holding his head high, he paced in the snow. Miracle's mother knew what that meant. Dropping her head into Greta's arms, the mother nuzzled as best she could, letting out a blow, a sound, as if to thank Greta for the love and care she'd given her baby. With sadness in her eyes, the mother hesitated and then joined the band. Surrounding Greta, they all paced in the snow until the lead stallion nodded his head. Turning, racing with the wind, the horses disappeared in a curtain of snow churning and twirling into the horizon.

No one budged. So much had happened so quickly.

Henry was the first to reach Greta. Picking her up, he held the little girl who'd stolen his heart. Words had no use for the moment. Greta was the first to break the silence.

"I know you're not Santa, Henry. But your eyes twinkle like Santa's, and you make me feel happy. But I don't feel happy right now."

As tears fell down their cheeks, Henry told Greta how happy and safe she'd made Miracle feel.

"You were like a mommy to Miracle. You took good care of him. You loved him. All the horses knew how much Miracle loved you."

"But I didn't say goodbye to Miracle."

"You didn't have to, Greta. Miracle will keep you in his heart."

Everyone reached the two huddled in a snowdrift about the same time. Everyone had tears in their eyes. Taking Greta in her arms, Meg kept telling her daughter how much she loved her.

"I will miss Miracle, Mommy."

"Miracle will miss you too, honey."

"Do you miss your Mommy?"

"Your mommy misses her mommy, Greta."

"Why doesn't my grandmother visit us? Maybe she would have loved Miracle, too."

"I'm going to call her soon, sweetheart. I'm sure she would have loved Miracle."

"We can show her pictures, right, Uncle Sammy?"

Sammy didn't know what to say. He'd shot all of what just unfolded but felt guilty doing it. Hugging Greta, he told her how sorry he was and how lucky she and Miracle had been to share time together. Then he added, "I won't do Miracle's story if you don't want me to, Greta."

"I want you to. Can I help you with Miracle's story?"

"I need you to help me. This will be your story too."

As everyone stayed clustered together comforting Greta in the cold, Teddy again made an obvious suggestion.

"Since tomorrow is Saturday, is there any reason to rush back today?"

The idea drifted about those gathered.

"I think you should stay one more night," said Steve.

"We could go to the restaurant for dinner," said Ben.

"And we could go on one more sleigh ride," added Henry.

"We haven't packed anything in the car. I think one more night is a great idea," said Ellie. "That is if you can stand us that long, Meg."

"It's a wonderful idea. Having family together is comforting."

"I have a suggestion," said Sammy. "Remember the pond Mom found when you moved here, Dad?"

"I remember. Abbey was so excited."

"We can shovel it off. Then go rent some skates."

"We'll have a day of skating and sleigh riding," said Maggie.

"Miracle would have liked that," said Greta.

"Then I declare this Miracle's Day," said Sammy.

"No need to rent skates, Mr. Sammy. We have whatever you might need."

"Why am I not surprised?"

"You know me, Mr. Steve."

"So do I," said Greta. "So did Miracle."

"Indeed, Miss Greta, indeed." With tears getting in his way, Thomas had to step back.

The family discussed plans and made reservations. After Bobby's nap, the day would unfold. The priority for everyone was making sure Greta felt their love and support. It's funny how loss can bring people together without saying a word. Holes in hearts need each other, as evident in majestic wild horses gathered around a little girl—all in need of comforting.

Chapter Twenty-One

THEIR EXTRA DAY TOGETHER PROVED TO be another one to remember. Teddy had never been on skates but that didn't stop him. Getting on the ice, Ben talked about going skating behind the orphanage.

"The rink was huge but then I was just a kid."

"Oh Benny, it was so huge," said Sophie, sitting in a chair wrapped up in blankets. "Sister Mary Beth made sure there was room for every one of us."

"What is an orphanage?" Greta asked.

"It's a big house with lots of children," Sophie explained.

That seemed to satisfy Greta as Sammy pulled her around the ice on a plastic sled.

After the skates were off and mittens dried, everyone went back outside. Thomas and Henry had the sleighs ready to go. Edmund joined them. This time they went in another direction, following the river that divided the back fields. When they made it to a plank bridge, Thomas slowed down.

"We'll go over one at a time, Henry."

Thomas waited for Henry to cross.

"This side seems like a different world."

"In some ways it is, Mr. Henry."

Thomas took off, still following the river. There were no farms. No thickets or pine trees. After going around a bend something could be seen in the distance sitting along the river's edge. They watched what seemed to be a structure of some sort getting closer. Going over a narrow creek frozen in place, Thomas pulled back on the reins. He kept that pace as they made their way through the entrance of a wrought iron fence left wide open. Instead of stopping, he went around what resembled a castle.

"The detail resembles that of something built during the French Renaissance. I've never seen such elaborate gables," said Ben. "What is this prime example of a French Chateau doing here?"

"It seems to be abandoned, Dad. I stayed in places like this when I was in France."

"While abandoned, Miss Maggie, it's considered a sacred place by the locals. Vandals have stayed away. Instead people come for the experience."

"What do you mean, Thomas?"

"I will show you, Miss Ellie."

Once the horses were secured, Sophie was helped out of the sleigh. Cate took pictures as she went along. After walking up a grand stairway, Thomas waited for everyone. Then, opening a wooden door, they entered what seemed to be a castle covered in layers of frost. Marble pillars and a marble staircase glimmered. Gold and silver fixtures glistened as the sun streaked through the windows.

"Does a princess live here?" Greta asked.

"No one lives here, Miss Greta."

"Breathtaking. It's like a scene out of *Dr. Zhivago*," said Ellie.

"I feel like I'm in Europe again," said Maggie. "There's artwork still on the walls. Furniture is still in place. It feels as if whoever lived here will be coming home any minute."

Thomas told the story behind the deserted structure by the river. "This was designed by and built for Frank Vincent. Because he was a bit of an eccentric, completion of the project took years. Mr. Vincent was a leader in the railroad industry. He and his wife, Agnes, had three children—two boys and a girl named Yvonne. The boys went to work in their father's company. Story goes Yvonne was strong-willed. She and her mother clashed more often than not. Frank proved to be not a nice man to the point Agnes left him. You must remember that was back when most women stayed married no matter the circumstances. But Agnes couldn't take it any longer. By all accounts, she gave up wealth for peace of mind. Despite Frank's actions being the reason for Agnes leaving, Yvonne blamed her mother. Sadly, Agnes died years later of a broken heart. More than anything, she'd wanted her daughter back in her life, but Yvonne never spoke to her mother again. Agnes never did find peace of mind."

"Such a tragedy," said Sophie. "Most every family struggles with hurt and anger and many fail to get beyond that point. So many years wasted."

"I believe I know why you brought us here, Thomas."

"I thought you would, Miss Meg."

"I'm surprised I never heard of this place," said Steve.

"Thinking back, I remember hearing a few references to Frank Vincent at the restaurant but I never knew the story behind the name," said Eric.

"Why didn't you tell me about the Vincent family before now?"

"You weren't ready to hear their story, Miss Meg."

"You are right, Thomas. But after listening to Greta tell Miracle's mother how a mommy's love is a special love and now hearing the tragic story of the Vincent family I am ready. I will be calling my mother tonight, Thomas. I pray I haven't allowed too much time to pass us by."

"You are taking the step. That warms my heart, Miss Meg. The rest is up to fate."

"Can we look around?" asked Sammy. "I'm seeing this place through the lens."

"Feel free to wander, Mr. Sammy. With well over two hundred acres connected to this magnificent structure, Mr. Vincent put it all into a trust before he passed away. A caretaker lives nearby. He's used to people stopping and taking photos. Some say they've seen Agnes's spirit up on one of the grand balconies but I have never seen her."

"To think I travel the world for story ideas and I find two when I'm home for Christmas."

"I dare say your senses are always on," said Henry.

After wandering through that silent castle, they headed back home. Dinner reservations were for five. They were early. Spending a good part of the day outside had made them hungry for a warm meal. It also made them tired. They made plans for the morning.

"No excuses tomorrow," said Ben. "We'll be on the road early."

It wasn't long before everyone had gone to bed—everyone except for Meg.

After changing into her nightgown, Meg sat on the edge of the bed. She couldn't stop the tears. Half asleep, Eric asked if she'd made the call.

"I was about to, but I keep crying."

Rolling over, Eric embraced his wife, whispering he understood the fear she must be feeling.

"I thought it was fear, but it's not."

"What do you mean, honey?"

"I'm remembering a Christmas after my parents divorced." Meg stopped for a second. No matter how old you get, painful memories still hurt.

"My mother had asked me to help her bake cookies for Santa. Instead of helping, I ran in my bedroom and slammed the door. Later on, while feeling sorry for myself, I could smell cookies baking. They smelled so good. I wanted some of those cookies but I wouldn't budge. When I woke up there was a plateful sitting on a chair beside my bed. I didn't eat a one but I wanted to. I would give anything to go back and change my actions that evening. How could I have been so mean to my mother?"

"When you're a little kid, you don't understand adult situations. You were hurt. You were confused, mad. I'm sure you were worried about your father, far away and alone. You missed being a family so you lashed out at your mother."

"I was so mean."

"Your world was shattered and the only adult around to blame was your mother."

"But I didn't even know why they divorced."

"Exactly, Meg. You were a child."

"I can't imagine the pain I caused."

"You were in pain."

"I don't want our children to have to experience that pain. We can't take anything for granted. You are my best friend. My best friend."

Pulling Meg even closer, Eric whispered, "You've put a meaning in my life I never thought possible."

Lingering as the crescent moon shed light into their bedroom, Eric brushed Meg's hair off her shoulders. Kissing her forehead and the nape of her neck, Eric's fingers tilted her lips to his. Their tender moment gave Meg the strength she needed.

"No matter her reaction," Eric whispered, "You are doing the right thing."

"But what if I'm too late?"

"But what if you're not?"

Remembering her brother's remark about their mother staying up late watching old movies, Meg thanked Eric for his encouragement. Kissing him tenderly, she got out of bed to search her phone for the number. Sitting in an old wicker rocker near a window looking out over the fields, Meg hesitated. She was so young when her parents divorced. She'd built a wall around herself to keep the hurt away. Now, blessed with her own family, Meg was ready to reach out to the one person she missed the most. With a deep breath, Meg placed the call and then sat there, waiting—the aroma of cookies baked long ago filling her with a longing for a woman she'd told herself was mean and calculating. Snow swirling in little whirlwinds over the fields sparkled in the moonlight.

One ring.

Two.

Each ring took a lifetime. About to hang up for fear of her mother being asleep, Meg's heart started pounding even harder when a voice at the other end said hello. Meg froze. So many images raced through her mind. So many memories came at her one right after another. In a split second her strength was waning. Doubts were back.

"Hello?"

The voice at the other end sounded weak. Meg reacted. "Hello . . . hello, Mom. This is Meg."

The silence on the other end was deafening. Remembering the strength Greta had shown spurred Meg on to try again.

"This is your daughter, Mom. It's me, Meg."

"Meg?"

"Yes. It's Meg. I"—clearing her throat, Meg noted one star in particular glittering a bit brighter than the rest. Meg was convinced it was Abbey. That's all she needed—"I wanted to call to wish you a Merry Christmas. I realize I've let so many holidays go by but I want to tell you I understand Mom. I know you did the best you could. I know that now."

With no reply, Meg kept talking. "I have two beautiful children and a remarkable husband. It's because of them that I've learned how hard it all is."

"Hard?"

That's all that came from the other end of the line. Silence took over until that voice now quivering asked again, "Hard? What do you mean by how hard it all is?"

"Being married, raising a family, keeping it all together. It's not easy to do under the best of circumstances. I know you had so much on your shoulders dealing with an alcoholic husband."

There! Meg said it. Her father had been an alcoholic. She said it. She put it out there. He too had flaws. He too held some responsibility in what had happened so many years ago.

"I never accused your father of being an alcoholic in front of you and your brother. I made a point of never saying one bad word about him. He was your father. You didn't need to hear me tearing him down. Dealing with a divorce was hard enough for the both of you."

"I understand that now, and I thank you for shielding us the best you could."

"Your father was the only man I ever loved. It was the addiction I divorced."

"I get that. You divorced out of love, if that makes any sense."

"It made sense to me. I had no choice, Meg. He wouldn't stop."

"Mom?"

"Yes, Meg."

"I wish I'd made cookies with you that night instead of running to my room and slamming the door."

"I realized later I was asking a lot of you."

"You remember that night?"

"Of course I do."

"I have to tell you how much I wanted to eat the cookies you left for me. They smelled so good."

"It was your grandmother's recipe."

"Your mother?"

"No—your father's"

"I don't remember much about my grandparents."

"When we divorced that was the end of any communication with your father's side. His mother had given me a cookbook when we were first married. She'd put stars next to her favorite recipes."

"Was French toast one of them? I loved your French toast although I'm sure I never told you."

"Yes. That was one of her recipes. The trick was the temperature of the skillet and using fresh eggs and lots of cinnamon."

"I liked it when you cooked French toast for supper."

"Those were the times when I was too tired to prepare anything else. I knew you and your brother were happy with French toast, and your father—well, it usually didn't matter with him. Most times he didn't eat with us anyway."

Not wanting to get too deep into the past, Meg told her mother she hoped she wasn't calling too late in the evening.

"Not at all. I've been watching Liz Taylor movies."

"Funny you should mention her. My husband gave me a collection of Taylor–Burton movies for Christmas a few years ago knowing how much I like their films."

"My favorite's *The Sandpiper*. I'm watching it again right now."

"I like that one, too. The chemistry those two had was written in their eyes. That was not acting."

"It takes more than chemistry to keep it together as evident in their private life."

"True. I'd be easy if that's all it took."

"I'd still be married. Your father and I did have that thing, that chemistry. It wasn't always bad, Meg."

"I wish I'd understood back then but as my husband reminds me, kids don't understand adult situations."

"More often than not adults don't either."

"Exactly what Eric said."

"Eric—is that your husband?"

"Yes. He tolerated me when I was at my worst."

"That's what it's about, Meg. That's how it's supposed to work."

"But I was out-of-control mean and cold when we lived in New York."

"The city can do that to people."

"I was doing it as an attorney during the day and taking it home with me in the evening."

"How did you turn it around?"

"Eric's mother opened my eyes and my heart. I'll never forget her telling me one Christmas morning that I'd never walked in your shoes. I didn't know what you were going through. She told me to let it go—told me to let life in and that's what I am doing. Eric's mother was a wise woman."

"You say she was a wise woman. Has she passed away, Meg?"

"Yes, sadly she passed away a year before Greta was born but her spirit remains a part of us."

"From what I can gather, your husband inherited his mother's intuitiveness."

"He has indeed. It's because of Eric's mother that he walked away from Wall Street."

"That takes courage."

"Abbey sensed his unhappiness. She reminded Eric of his passion for cooking."

"That was the spark?"

"Yes it was the spark. Now he owns his own restaurant and loves every minute of it."

"That proves the difference between a job and a passion."

"Eric collected cookbooks when he was young. His mother saved all of them. Eric never understood why she did that until we had children."

"Tell me about your children, Meg."

For the next fifteen minutes or so, Meg talked about Greta and Bobby. She could have kept going but realized the hour.

"It's late, Mom, and you're missing your movie."

"I know every word. I've watched it so many times."

"Mind if I call you again?"

"I'd like that, Meggie."

"Meggie?"

"I'm sorry. It slipped out. That's what your father and I would call you, especially when tucking you into bed at night."

The tears were back. Meg wanted to be that little girl again. She realized that however grown up she sounded, she still kept a part of that little girl inside her. She still missed them being together, being a family, and being tucked into bed. But she kept all of that to herself.

"Maybe the kids and I could come visit you?"

"I think that would be lovely. I'll make French toast."

"And down the road, I'd love to have you visit us for as long as possible."

"We can discuss that when you come. Meg . . ."

"Yes, Mom?"

"Thank you for calling."

"I'm sorry it took me so long."

"That doesn't matter, honey. That doesn't matter."

They said good night.

Sitting in that old rocker, Meg's tears fell as freely as the snowflakes drifting by the bedroom window. As the crescent moon appeared from behind the clouds, Eric was by her side. Without hesitating, he scooped Meg up in his arms and carried her to their bed.

"She loves me, Eric. I know she loves me. I felt it."

"I'm certain your mother has always loved you, my darling."

As the wind whipped the snow up and around, their passions played out, stirring the night.

Chapter Twenty-Two

BEN WANTED TO BE ON THE road early so Eric was in the kitchen by six. While getting what he needed out of a cupboard, he mulled over something Meg had said before drifting off to sleep: "I felt your mother beside me every minute I was on the phone."

Rubbing his fingers around the rim of the old cracked bowl he'd always use, Eric remembered a conversation he and Abbey had the first Christmas in the farmhouse. As he was cracking eggs, Eric had remarked about the bowl he was using—the same one he was now holding.

"This is your mom's bowl."

"How did you remember?" she'd asked.

"It has a little crack. I used to think when I'd break open eggs, I'd break the bowl. It has to be ancient."

"It goes back a few generations. I only use it during the holidays."

"Did your Mom do that? Save it for the holidays?"

"I don't know, Eric. It's what I choose to do."

So much had changed since that Christmas. Meg was right. It was all because of Abbey whose resentment toward her mother held inside for years afforded her insight into Meg's feelings toward *her* mother. Cracking eggs on the rim of that old bowl, Eric thanked his mother. She'd turned his life into living instead of existing.

"Did you hear me, honey?" asked Meg. "I said good morning."

"You have me thinking of my mother."

"I do?"

"You were falling asleep when you told me you felt her beside you while you were on the phone."

"I don't remember saying that. For some reason, I was exhausted," smiled Meg. "But it's the truth. Abbey never left my side."

"Come here, sweetheart. I need a kiss. I seem to be a little exhausted myself."

"That's the sort of exhaustion I love," whispered Meg, wrapped up in her husband's arms.

"I'm proud of you for calling your mother."

"I miss her this morning more than ever. Did I tell you we both love Liz Taylor movies? I found that amazing."

"Must be in the genes. Mom and I shared a love for poetry, specifically Robert Frost. I never knew she had any interest until one day when I was in high school. I came home reciting Frost."

"Good morning. Don't mean to eavesdrop," said Henry, walking into the kitchen, "but poetry is the song of the heart."

"Henry knows what he is talking about," said Sophie, standing in the doorway. Adjusting a hair comb, Sophie took her time getting to the coffee.

"You are one lucky woman," said Eric.

"Indeed." Henry laughed, looking out the back door. "Weather looks good."

"Forecast has it clear all the way."

"You could always hitch that sleigh of yours to the back of the van just in case it turns."

"You don't know how much I'd love to do that, Meg. The sleigh is a beauty. But I'm afraid Thomas would miss it after all the work he put into it."

"I remember Thomas saying it is your sleigh," said Eric.

"I'm certain he meant the sleigh was mine to use during our visit."

"And what a visit it's been," said Sophie. "I've loved every minute. If you don't mind, I'm taking my coffee and going in to sit by the tree one last time."

"I'll be right behind you, honey. Just want to grab some jam tarts."

"They're fresh out of the oven, Henry. Tarts were first on my list to bake this morning."

"I could tell by the aroma. Thank you for taking the time to make them again."

"It's the simple things that mean the most."

"So true, Meg." Filling a small plate, Henry went to sit with Sophie as Greta and Bobby came rushing in to the kitchen.

Once everyone was downstairs, they gathered around the dining-room table. Dishes were passed and refilled. Compliments to the chef kept coming.

"What is your secret with these delicious waffles, Eric?"

"I mixed in leftover pumpkin from the pies. Once they were done, I drizzled honey butter over them. The maple syrup is local."

"You can taste the difference in the syrup."

"I was there when the syrup was boiled down, Ben. A neighbor has been doing it for years," said Steve.

"We could start tapping the maples. It wouldn't take much to put a shack up behind your place," said Henry.

"I've thought about doing that, Dad. We'll add it to our list of projects."

While they enjoyed a last cup of coffee together, the conversation turned to what had taken place over the last few days.

"Teddy and I will never be able to thank you for opening up your home to us—not only for the wedding but also for Christmas," said Maggie. "The sleigh rides, the barns, the marshmallows, the horses—all priceless memories."

"It was more than I ever anticipated," said Meg, holding Eric's hand.

"When Maggie and I started talking about a double wedding, I didn't think about the impact the setting would have. You can't top what we had for atmosphere."

"I had my doubts but I agree with you, Sammy," said Teddy.

A knock at the back door interrupted the moment.

"Good morning, Thomas. Good morning, Edmund," said Steve.

"Come in and join us. We're talking about the good time we shared and you two played a role in all of it."

This time Thomas didn't refuse Steve's invitation. He and Edmund had a cup of coffee. Thomas even had a waffle.

"Mr. Steve and I were in on the making of the syrup. I must say it is indeed delicious as is the waffle, Mr. Eric."

"Thanks, Thomas. Come for breakfast anytime."

"Miss Meg has her hands full. But I felt this was a special occasion."

"I was going to go to the barn to thank you, Thomas. I'll drive a sleigh alongside you any day," Henry said.

"It's been a pleasure to meet another who shares a love of sleighs. I too have found your visit a memorable one."

"Steve tells me you're going home in a few days. Where exactly is that? I'm assuming you get one heck of a winter wherever it is."

"We do get one heck of a winter, Mr. Henry."

That was the extent of Thomas's answer. Henry didn't push it. He'd come to understand Thomas was a private individual.

It wasn't long before Ben brought them back to reality.

"I know we'd prefer to sit here all day, but we'd better get on the road. Never can tell what's ahead."

As they found their coats and boots and gathered whatever else was left upstairs, Ben went out and started the car. Once Sophie was settled in the back, holding close the old box shaped like a heart, hugs and tears were nonstop.

"We'll see you at our reception in May," said Maggie.

"Then we'll see you at ours in LA in October," said Cate.

"Sophie and I love October," said Henry. "That was the month of our wedding."

"Too bad there won't be any snow," said Steve.

"You never can be certain about that," said Henry with that twinkle in his eye.

Picking Greta up and giving her a big Santa hug, Henry told her what a good girl she was and how blessed the wild horses were to have her as a friend.

"Wild horses never allow anyone to pet them, Greta. They know how much you loved Miracle."

"I love all the horses. And I love you too, Henry."

Going down the driveway, Henry shouted one last ho-ho-ho as Ben made the turn and they disappeared around the bend.

Chapter Twenty-Three

The farmhouse seemed quiet even with Bobby and Greta playing in the front room.

"It went by so fast," said Meg, putting stuff away in the kitchen.

"Thanks for everything you did. Dad would have been overwhelmed pulling it all together."

"I had fun, Sammy. I'd suggest what I thought we should do and your father went along with everything."

"That's because your suggestions were good ones," said Steve, coming in to the room with his old work coat on.

Thanking Steve, Meg went to check on the kids.

"Where are you headed, Dad?"

"Out to chop some wood."

"Want some help?"

"No. After all I've eaten, I need the exercise."

"I know what you mean. I think Greta and I will be skating later."

"That sounds like fun," said Cate. "Then maybe we can start looking at all the shots we took of the horses."

"You read my mind. I'm relying on Greta's input on this project."

"Greta will give it to you straight," said Eric, pulling a large pan out from the cupboard. "Dinner will be about six, Dad."

"Did I mention I'm going to Susan's for dinner? She leaves tomorrow for Maine."

Hearing Steve mention another woman's name other than Abbey's, it took a moment for those present to adjust their thinking.

"Okay, Dad. I'll save you some dessert. I'm attempting Mom's famous chocolate sauce."

"Over vanilla ice cream?" Steve asked.

"Definitely."

"I can't believe you've never made that before."

"It's not the easiest thing to make, Sammy. I can still see Mom standing at the stove and stirring the sauce until it thickened."

"Your mother learned the hard way, boys. It took her a few tries to perfect that sauce."

Grabbing his gloves, Steve went out the back door. The sun against the snow made it hard to see. It didn't stop him. Steve could do this routine in his sleep. As he split the wood, a Christmas of long ago came to mind. Abbey was in the kitchen of their small apartment in Charleston. She was excited to try a recipe she'd found in a cookbook that had been her mother's. She'd told Steve it was going to be a surprise. As he was stringing lights on a tree that took up the entire living room, Steve could smell something burning. Rushing in to the kitchen he found Abbey at the sink with the water running and tears streaming down her cheeks.

"Are you okay, honey? Did you burn yourself?"

The tears kept coming. Abbey couldn't speak. Checking to make sure the burners were off, Steve held her as the water kept flowing into a pot still steaming.

A few minutes later, Abbey whispered she was sorry.

"For what?"

"For burning your surprise."

"As long as you are okay, nothing else matters."

After a few more minutes, Abbey explained. "I know how much you love chocolate. I was going to make you a chocolate sauce for dessert tonight. Instead I ruined a pot and wasted money we don't have."

"There are other pots and we have so many dinners ahead of us. I love you for thinking of me and my chocolate urge."

Turning the water off, Steve picked Abbey up in his arms. "Now speaking of urges," he said. Carrying her into the bedroom, they made love as the aroma of burned chocolate circled a tree that was half decorated.

A few weeks later Abbey surprised Steve with the best chocolate sauce he'd ever tasted. And over the years she kept surprising him even when it wasn't a special occasion.

AROUND 3:30, STEVE LEFT FOR SUSAN'S house. He'd never been to her place. She'd invited him a few times but he had declined. When Susan asked him again Christmas night he thought for a moment and then accepted. Taking the left off 93, Steve kept driving until he saw the white fence about a mile in. Susan told him her place was the Quaker-style home with a cranberry door down on the right. Even though the sun was setting, the door stood out due to the small lights around its frame. Walking up the few steps, Steve rang the bell.

When the door opened and Susan was standing there smiling, her eyes as green as shamrocks, it was as if Steve was looking at her for the first time.

"Welcome, Steve. Please come in."

"Thank you. Your home is charming."

Taking Steve's coat, Susan explained how she and her husband had been adamant in keeping as much of the original architecture intact.

"Many would have replaced a lot of what you see but we felt it all added to the appeal."

"Ben told me he believes buildings have a way of talking to us. The older they get, the louder they speak."

"I believe that. This place was in shambles, yet Paul and I saw its beauty underneath years of neglect."

"Was Paul in construction at some point?"

"No. He loved history. Any sort of history, whether it was a building, person, or country, Paul respected its place in the universe even if the history was appalling. It was all one big story to him."

"That makes sense with him being an editor."

"Paul was of the old-school type of reporter-turned-editor. He'd go after the story instead of waiting for it to come to him."

"So much has changed," said Steve, remembering he was holding on to a gift bag. While he was an adult, he felt like an awkward teenager on his first date.

"I brought you something."

"How thoughtful. You didn't have to bring a thing, Steve."

"I wanted to, Susan."

Leading the way into a front room with a fireplace made of what appeared to be the original bricks accented by a narrow wooden mantle, Susan sat down on a mustard-colored sofa. Sitting beside her, Steve watched while Susan unwrapped a small, ceramic tree. He explained.

"When I saw it in a store window I remembered your comment about not putting a tree up because you'd be leaving for Maine. I believe everyone needs a tree."

"Thank you, Steve. It's perfect. I'll put it on the table while we have dinner."

"But wait. This tree is a magical tree."

He pushed a button underneath and the little tree lit up.

"Now it feels like Christmas. It's the first year this home has been without any sort of a tree. But then it's also the first year I'll be spending the winter in Maine without Paul."

"Are you hesitant?"

"It will be strange. While my children will visit off and on, most of the time it will be me with my sketch pads and canvas."

"The landscape must stimulate you as an artist."

"It does, along with the solitude."

"I'd venture to say many couldn't stand the solitude."

"I think you're right. With everyone so wired, solitude would be overwhelming. I'm looking forward to it. I have more than enough projects to keep me busy."

"You're quite an accomplished artist."

"It took years, Steve. I'm still learning. Things change so quickly with the technology."

"But technology can't replace the talent."

"True. Come with me. I'll show you my studio." Lingering on the sofa, Susan whispered, "I love my Christmas tree."

Walking into the dining room, Susan set the tree down on the dark oak table. While she went to a corner cupboard for wine glasses, Steve pushed that little tree's button. Twinkling colors spread out over the lace tablecloth. Taking a bottle of wine off the rack, Susan handed it to Steve.

"Would you mind opening it?"

"My pleasure."

A few seconds later, glasses were filled. Taking hold of Steve's hand, Susan led him down a hallway past what seemed to be a room full of books on shelves surrounding a roll top desk.

"Paul's office," was all Susan said.

Opening French doors leading to an area with more windows than walls, Susan told Steve how they'd torn down what had been nothing more than a shed and built her studio in its place.

"Paul made certain the studio blended into the framework of what was here."

"It reminds me of when Thomas and I added on to the farmhouse. It'd been Abbey's idea. Her concern was it might take away from what was in place. She'd be pleased how it turned out."

"I never saw your home without that room. If you hadn't told me, I would have assumed it'd been part of the original structure."

"Abbey would have loved this studio," said Steve walking around the easel and paints—tubes and brushes.

"I spent a long time in the design. Lighting is so important."

"If Abbey hadn't been so sick I might have considered adding sky-lights to the porch. With the trees, the sun was blocked more often than not. But then art wasn't a career for her. It was more of a hobby."

"From what I've seen of her paintings, Abbey was quite talented."

"She inherited that from her mother," said Steve, walking toward a back window. "The view is breathtaking, Susan."

"This time of the day and in early morning—especially in the win-ter—the view stops me cold. It stirs the juices."

"I'm not an artist but I can understand what you are saying," said Steve still looking outside as snow started falling and the sun disappeared for another day.

"You're far away, Steve."

"Just thinking how life throws us curve balls and we find ourselves on a path we never anticipated."

"Like being here with me?"

"Yes," replied Steve, turning, looking at Susan. "I never imagined my life without Abbey. I know I shouldn't be saying that but for some reason I feel comfortable in telling you."

"I understand what you mean. Paul was my only love. When he passed away, I considered that part of my life over."

Moving closer to Susan, Steve continued. "Now, being here, spending time with you—there is no guilt. No longing for the past."

"It feels like part of a plan greater than you or I can understand. Funny thing about that is Paul was never one to plan for the inevitable. He was so busy chasing the truth that he left that up to fate."

"That must have been hard on you, having him out there fighting the fight."

"Ironically, that's what attracted me to him back in the sixties when unrest was constant. Paul was a whirlwind yet in command. When Kennedy was assassinated, he didn't sleep for a week. He demanded every paper published told the story as accurately as possible for the sake of history."

"Sounds like Paul was a man of conviction."

"He was indeed. I think you and I were blessed, Steve. We married the loves of our lives and over the years our marriages stayed strong. I remember when our first child was born. Paul was on his way out the door to cover some unfolding story as my water broke. We were living outside of DC with no family nearby."

"So what did Paul do?"

"He grabbed my bag, called the doctor, and brought me to the hospital. By then I was having slight contractions so they admitted me. Paul asked the nurses to take good care of me, saying he'd be right back. He had a way with people. That's how he built up his list of informants. They all wanted to tell him what they knew."

"Were you upset about being in labor for your first child and being alone?"

"That's where the understanding kicked in. He told me when he proposed that being a reporter defined him. I knew he loved me. That's all that mattered. I later learned he'd given the doctor a heads-up on a story he was working on concerning pending state budget cuts that would affect the hospital. The doctor appreciated Paul's determination to expose what others in politics were trying to hide so the doctor never left my side."

"Did he make it back to the hospital on time?"

"Yes, he did. When I went in to labor for our second child, he was covering the Watergate hearings. I couldn't reach him so a neighbor took me to the hospital. I called the paper to let them know. I'll never forget Paul's face when he stormed into the delivery room the moment our son was born."

"Some stories write their own headlines, Susan."

"Yes. I found that out the hard way."

Putting her glass down, Susan rubbed her arms as she turned toward the windows.

"Are you cold?"

When Susan didn't answer, Steve put his glass down as well and went to her side. Without speaking, he wrapped her up in his arms as the wind moved the snow in circles.

"Want to go back and sit by the fire while you get warm?"

After a few seconds Susan whispered she just needed a minute. When she was ready, she explained her silence.

"I apologize for my reacting."

"Reacting?"

"When you said some stories write their own headlines I thought of Paul's final story."

Steve sensed it'd be best if he let Susan speak at her own pace. And that is what she did.

"Sadly," Susan continued, "Paul's final story was about his death. Run over by a drunk driver while he was covering a fire. By then he was an editor, but when a call came in, he jumped."

"How tragic. I am so sorry, Susan. I didn't know."

"It still hits me out of the blue sometimes. To think that such a man of integrity became the headline of such an insane act."

"That won't be Paul's final story. He left his mark both in print and with you and your family."

Looking into the night while still in Steve's arms, Susan considered what Steve had said. When you're so close to the hurt and pain, the goodness escapes the moment until it's pointed out by another.

"I never thought about it that way. You're right Steve. With his by-lines and reputation, Paul is a part of history and history was what Paul was all about."

"And you helped make that happen. We were lucky, Susan. Abbey understood me in the same way."

"I propose a toast to understanding." Picking up their glasses—raising them as the snow fell and the moon drifted through the clouds, the two shared a moment. It became their moment. No words were spoken yet so much was said. Surrounded by brushes, palettes, canvas, and inspiration, the moment intensified. Taking Susan's glass, Steve set it down next to his on a table full of sketches on paper. Holding her hand, Steve led Susan to the farthest corner of the studio. Moving strands of hair away from her face, Steve took her in his arms and held her as the snow circled outside. Pulling Susan even closer, Steve moved his fingers through her hair and gently, ever so gently, kissed her. Outside the wind was picking up. It went unnoticed. Dinner was a little late. It didn't matter. That little ceramic Christmas tree warmed two hearts as they lingered at the table. When he was leaving, the snow coming through the opened door didn't matter either as they said good night repeatedly.

"You are welcome any time in Portland."

Kissing her forehead and then tracing her lips with his fingers, Steve whispered, "I wouldn't want to interrupt your creative flow."

"I feel quite creative at the moment."

"They say absence makes the heart grow fonder."

"Then I can't wait for spring!"

"Thank you for a memorable evening, Susan."

Steve wanted to say more as he brought his lips to hers. He wanted to stay. He wanted to, but he didn't.

Chapter Twenty-Four

NEW YEAR'S EVE HAD ARRIVED WHEN it seemed like Christmas was just yesterday. Steve found it hard to believe he'd be saying goodbye to Thomas in a few hours. With Greta helping Sammy and Cate go through the photos and videos of the wild horses, the days had flown by. Susan was safe and sound in Portland. She and Steve talked just about every evening.

As Steve was getting a quick supper together, the phone rang.

"Good to hear from you, Henry. I was going to call you later. Yes. Okay. Great."

This time Henry's call was a short one unlike the night before last when he called after finding the sleigh Thomas had refurbished for him sitting inside his barn. At first Henry had some concern in how he'd explain it to Sophie. After talking it over with Steve, Henry figured out he'd tell her the truth.

"We don't keep secrets," Henry explained. "Sophie will believe me when I tell her about Santa Claus and how the sleigh ended up in our barn."

When asked what else was going on, Henry told him about a letter that was waiting for them when they got back home.

"It was postmarked Quebec—dated a month ago. It was from Sophie's great niece, Aubree, informing her Lily had passed away in late fall. Sophie was told she'd been in poor health for quite some time."

Henry explained Aubree was the granddaughter of a brother named Theodore—a brother Sophie did not remember. Aubree promised Lily she would try to find out what had happened to Sophie upon her passing. To her surprise, Aubree discovered Sophie's whereabouts scribbled on a legal pad in her father's desk drawer. He'd made a fortune in the oil industry. He never agreed with his family disowning Sophie. Once he retired, he employed an agency to find her. When they did he never contacted her. Aubree was certain her father would have if necessary. But that wasn't the end of the conversation.

"Aubree made mention of some family photos Lily kept in an old worn box with a gold clasp and how it had been her wish that Sophie— if found—be given the box upon her passing. Aubree went on to say the box had been misplaced by family members and should it be found she would send it along."

Henry told Steve how Sophie was now obsessed in finding out how the box ended up in that satchel at the exact same time she was in that barn in the woods.

"I would be too, Henry," said Steve. "All I can think is a certain someone made sure Lily's wish was granted."

The next morning Steve mentioned the situation concerning the box to Thomas. After Steve explained Henry's concerns and Sophie's obsession, Thomas simply replied, "Santa sees and hears things on his journey. In time, his actions will be explained and those who believe will understand."

Steve asked if that explanation might be coming soon for Sophie's sake. Thomas never answered. He went off to feed the reindeer.

After setting the table, Steve went in to the front room to tell the documentary makers dinner was ready. Finding them still hard at work, Steve asked how the project was coming along.

"I can see it, Dad. The photos, the videos, Greta and Miracle, and those stallions—it will touch heartstrings at any age."

"What's your timeline?"

"I'll know more once I get back."

"Uncle Sammy told me everyone will fall in love with Miracle, just like I did."

"And they'll fall in love with you, Greta, just like I did."

"You're my Grandpa, silly!"

"Aren't I the lucky one!"

"I was thinking, Dad. This could have the same appeal as the film we did on the untold stories between birthdate and death on tombstones. It's the human element again."

"I considered your mother's obsession with obituaries unique. From the response your work received, it was a testament to your mother's own human spirit."

"I agree, Dad. She was the driving force, just as Greta is for Miracle's story."

"With your creativeness flowing, I thought you three might be hungry. Meg and Bobby are on their way downstairs to join us. Since it's New Year's Eve, we won't be seeing Eric until well after midnight."

"Because we've been so busy we haven't made any plans for tonight."

"As your wife, I'd prefer a quiet New Year's Eve with my husband."

"That sounds good to me, honey. What are doing tonight , Dad? Too bad Susan is in Maine."

"I spoke with Susan earlier. She sends everyone her best wishes for the new year. As far as tonight, I'm going with Thomas to the barn in the woods. It will be his last evening here."

"I didn't realize he was leaving so soon," said Sammy. "I wanted to show him some of the video when he was driving the sleigh alongside the band of horses."

"Thomas has family responsibilities to tend to back home. But he'll be back. You will have that opportunity."

"Do you feel Edmund can step in to his shoes?" asked Cate.

"If anyone could it would be Edmund. But not even Edmund will ever be able to replace him. Thomas is one of a kind. I remember Abbey telling me there was something curious about him after their first meeting in the barn."

"Why do you think they became so close?"

Steve had to stop and think before answering his son's question.

How do you explain a bond most never realize? How do you sum up the trust, comfort, and love two strangers find almost instantly while being surrounded by reindeer? What they had was magical, reindeer and all.

"Thomas once told me Abbey was a believer, and believers see possibility. Thomas sees possibility. That was their bond. They felt it instantly. On the night your mother passed away, Thomas never left the reindeer. He slept on a bed of hay. He told me when he woke up the next morning, the reindeer surrounded him."

The wind seemed to pick up as Greta climbed into Steve's lap.

"Do reindeer cry, Grandpa?"

"I'm not sure."

"I saw tears in Miracle's mommy's eyes."

"Maybe it was the wind in her eyes."

"No. They were tears. Animals get sad too, Grandpa. Miracle's mommy missed him like I still do. I don't like feeling sad."

"If you remember all the fun you and Miracle had together, that sadness will turn into happy memories."

"Do you remember all the fun you and Grandma had?"

"I remember every moment we shared, Greta."

It wasn't long before they were sitting around the dining room table enjoying Steve's casserole and corn bread. Meg ate in a hurry. Bobby was cranky. Taking him upstairs for his bath, she told Greta to go up when she finished her supper.

"What time are you meeting Thomas, Dad?"

"I told him I'd be at the barn by six. Weather looks good."

"Can I go with you, Grandpa?"

"Not tonight, honey."

"I want to say goodbye to Thomas."

"I'm certain he has plans to stop by in the morning."

"I didn't get to say goodbye to Miracle."

"I'll make sure Thomas stops before he goes."

"Will Edmund let me feed my runt?"

"Yes, you will be able to feed your runt."

Once they enjoyed the rest of Eric's chocolate sauce over vanilla ice cream, Sammy insisted Steve get on his way.

"Cate and I will clean up and start to gather our stuff."

"We still have tomorrow."

"That we do, Dad."

After reminding Greta that her mother wanted her upstairs, Steve went out the back door. With a light snowfall and the moon shades of silvery blue, it was a perfect evening for a sleigh ride. While sure of his decision as to who would eventually follow in the role of the reindeer keeper's helper, Steve wondered what Thomas's reaction would be. Steve had spent a considerable amount of time going over his choices. Each had strong points. In his gut, Steve felt he'd made the best choice.

Chapter Twenty-Five

THERE WAS SOMETHING ESPECIALLY ENCHANTING ABOUT the old barn set off in a field in the wintertime, when the stars and moon were out, making the frosted panes look more like framed pieces of art, as if a great master had etched astonishing designs in each. No two were alike. Together they seemed to enhance the aura of that endearing place full of horses and reindeer and old sleighs linked to a never-ending story.

Steve found Thomas way in the back, where those sleighs were kept and cared for with the dignity they deserved.

"Something told me you'd still be at it, Thomas."

"I remember telling Miss Abbey the reindeer keeper's duties are never done. I've instilled that work ethic in Edmund. He's well-versed in the history he will be representing and understands the importance of his role. The reindeer respond to him in a respectful manner which means they will be ready if chosen."

"I never doubted you'd prepare Edmund for his role as reindeer keeper. I feel comfortable in his abilities. It's our friendship that's irreplaceable."

"A true friendship never goes away."

"Again, you simply state the truth."

"The truth is simple. People complicate the truth, Mr. Steve."

After taking one last look at the sleigh he'd been polishing, Thomas polished the runners of another.

"This one is particularly meaningful to you, Mr. Steve. I had to check to make sure."

Steve didn't say a word. He felt that childhood wonder stir deep inside. It's always inside us. It never goes away.

"After Santa delivered your father back to Korea, he had to replace this sleigh. It'd been a dangerous journey but one he was determined to complete."

"My father—you mean my father sat in this sleigh?"

"Indeed, Mr. Steve. Indeed he did right alongside Santa Claus."

In an instant Steve was that seven-year-old boy waiting for Santa to bring his father home for Christmas from a war halfway around the world. He knew Santa would bring him home. Steve had written him a letter. He remembered every word—"Please bring my Daddy home for Christmas. He is far away in a war. Daddy always takes me sledding down the big hill the day after Christmas. My sisters go too. I know Daddy will be sad if he can't take us."

Getting closer to the sleigh, Steve took his gloves off and moved his hands along its side and then around the back and along the other side. As he remembered that early morning, his bedroom door opening and those familiar footsteps walking toward his bed, Steve climbed up onto the sleigh. He was certain he could smell licorice cough drops as tears fell.

Realizing Steve needed time to himself, Thomas went outside to check on Edmund who was hitching up the horses. Throwing extra blankets in the back of the sleigh, Thomas asked Edmund for his assistance. He led his son into the toolshed stocked full with parts and bits and pieces.

"I've been waiting for the right moment to give you this, Edmund. I will be taking my last ride tonight as reindeer keeper. Tomorrow I pass that honor on to you."

Thomas handed Edmund never before used reindeer reins. "They are designed for the reindeer keeper—and only for the reindeer keeper."

"Thank you, Father. I will not let you down."

As they were coming out of the shed, Steve was walking back from the many sleighs lined up one after another. He and Thomas shared a smile. That's all that was needed. Dimming the lights and checking in on the reindeer, Thomas stated it was time to go.

"Sit with me, Mr. Steve. Edmund can sit in the back for one last time. Enjoy the ride, son!"

Off they went over the fields and around thickets. With the heavens full of glistening stars and that blue-tinted moon shining, the landscape resembled that of a snow globe—all shook up and glistening. The horses didn't need direction. Instinct told them where they were headed. Once into the woods, Thomas slowed their pace. Lanterns high in the trees led them to their destination, lit up and waiting for their arrival.

"I'll take care of the horses, Father, while you and Mr. Steve get comfortable inside."

"You're going to miss him, aren't you?"

"Terribly I'm afraid, Mr. Steve. While showing emotion is not one of our usual traits, being a parent does cause a tear now and then."

Everything was set. The tree lights were on. The lanterns lit. And again, it was warm. Steve knew better than to ask how.

"I have some tea ready to be made, Mr. Steve, if you'd like a cup. There's something soothing about a cup of tea when sitting down for a conversation with a good friend."

"I agree. I'd enjoy a cup while sharing time with you."

Thomas pushed the door open to the side room and heated the water. Then he put the tea bags in the cups.

"Miss Abbey always chose this particular cup and saucer."

"I can see why. The flowers resemble some she'd painted."

"I thought the same. Tonight the cup will be yours."

Sitting by the tree decked in glass bulbs next to that original sleigh with that famous satchel, the two friends began sharing thoughts and concerns, hopes and dreams. When Edmund walked in they didn't stop. Even when he came back with a cup of tea and sat down nearby, they continued.

"I am not disappearing, Mr. Steve. I won't be far away. There comes a time to step aside. One feels it in one's heart. Our existence is forever evolving. That's how we grow."

"I get it. If we don't accept that fact we remain stuck. I've come to realize we keep the memories in our heart as we move ahead."

"It makes me happy to hear you say that, Mr. Steve. Keep moving forward. Miss Abbey will forever be with you."

Steve was going to explain how even though he realized that, moving on was hard to do. Steve had listened to Ben and others giving him advice. He grasped all that he heard. But for Steve, moving on was a struggle. It had nothing to do with Susan. In fact, Steve felt strongly attracted to her. He'd wanted to stay the night after having dinner with her before she left for Maine. The chemistry was there. That was something that needed no explaining. And now that she was gone, he missed seeing her. If he was honest with himself, he was afraid. It wasn't as if he was still a teenager. He wondered if he had it in him to step back out there. If only he could be certain this was that moment. If only he could be certain he and Susan were meant to be.

A rumbling outside interrupted the conversation. Edmund jumped up to see what was going on. Before he made it halfway, the door opened. In stepped Henry with Sophie leaning on her cane.

Chapter Twenty-Six

"Didn't know if we'd make it! Didn't know if I'd get that sleigh off the ground, but those horses of mine proved me wrong. Once they built up speed, we were flying!"

Taking his hat off and pulling his scarf down, Henry shook the snow away. With his arm around Sophie, who was holding on to her cane, he led her toward the tree. Steve jumped up to meet them. Edmund grabbed blankets and made them a warm place on one of the benches. Then he went to check the horses as Thomas hurried to greet their visitors. Once Henry was comfortable, he started talking.

"I figured it out, Steve."

"Figured it out?"

"Figured out why that sleigh was in my barn. It's supposed to get me back here, back to this barn. I told you Sophie and I don't keep secrets. I told her. Told her everything, and she believed me, Steve."

"I'm not surprised, Henry."

"This believer hasn't slept well since learning of my sister's passing. The letter I received mentioned an old blue box with a gold clasp and my sister's wish to have me found and be given the box. The letter also stated it came up missing for some unexplainable reason. I need to know how the box found its way into that satchel sitting beside you, Thomas. It has to be Lily's box. It was full of photos of our family. Even though my family rejected me, I still need to connect with anything linked to Lily."

Henry pulled Sophie close to him. "I know you have the answers, Thomas. Why was that box in that satchel? Whose satchel is it? Why is it here?"

"I will answer your questions. But first I have a few of my own."

"Fair enough," said Henry.

"You feel the sleigh was given to you so you'd be able to return here?"

"I do. There could be no other reason."

"Why do you say that?"

"I am aware of the purpose of this place. I can't explain it, but I feel a connection. That sleigh is not an ordinary sleigh. It was given to me to keep that connection should it be necessary that I be here. That's what I felt earlier today. It was as if we were being pulled back here tonight."

"You are a wise man, Henry."

"Wisdom comes from living, Thomas."

"True. So you hitched your horses up to the sleigh and believed they would fly you here?"

"I believed they would because I knew in my heart they could."

"What would you have done if they couldn't?"

"That was never an option. I needed to get Sophie the answers she deserves so I trusted in the horses getting us back here. You are the key to Sophie finding resolution. She's been through enough. She's given all her life."

"I understand the good Miss Sophie has done. When you said you told her everything, I am to surmise that included Santa Claus?"

"Yes, and after I told Sophie about the sleigh and meeting Santa Claus, she told me she'd written Santa a letter earlier this month asking him to find Lily."

"Why did you write Santa Claus, Miss Sophie? You are an adult writing to Santa Claus?"

"While living at the orphanage, I learned there is a Santa Claus."

"How so?"

"The last Christmas the orphanage was open, we celebrated at a camp used in the summer. It was down in the woods just like this place so we went in by sleighs. When we were leaving, we found ourselves surrounded by reindeer. They were magnificent. There were so many that I lost count. Once the horses started moving, the reindeer did the same. When the horses picked up speed, the reindeer picked up speed. They stayed with us until we were out of the woods."

"So because reindeer followed you out of the woods, you believe there is a Santa Claus, Miss Sophie?"

"We were a family of orphans. I, being one of the oldest, took many of the younger orphans under my wing. I found myself caring about them. I knew their stories. When those reindeer appeared out of nowhere and followed us to the edge of the woods, I saw magic in so many of the children's eyes, magic where sadness often crept in at Christmas time, for that's when the reality of not having a family and a home hit the hardest. Santa Claus sent those reindeer. I know he did. I felt it in my heart."

"Tell Thomas about Johnny," said Henry.

"Johnny was a character. He always wore suspenders even in the summer. Because he was blind it was understood there was little chance anyone would adopt him. But a few months before that particular Christmas a couple took to him. They started the adoption procedure. Johnny was over-the-moon excited. We were excited for him. His adopted mother-to-be would visit every day. She'd describe their home in detail, especially the room that would be his bedroom. At supper, Johnny would tell us how the window in his bedroom overlooked the garden and when the weather was nice, he'd be able to open the window and smell the flowers and apple trees. They made plans for him to go to specialists, made plans on adding a swing set in the backyard, and talked about taking him to ballgames. Five days before Christmas Johnny was summoned to the office. He was told the couple had stopped the adoption process for no apparent reason. We later found out the woman was expecting a baby—a baby doctors told them they'd never be able to conceive."

Thomas had to sit down. His face went white. Although he was not to show emotion, he couldn't stop a few tears from falling. Minutes later he asked one more question.

"What was Johnny's reaction to the reindeer, Miss Sophie?"

By now, everyone had tears in their eyes. Henry handed Sophie his handkerchief. With the blue moon enhancing the stained-glass windows, that barn took on a most enchanting feeling—a feeling of magic and reindeer and believing in the wonder of it all.

"Many of the reindeer surrounded Johnny when he walked out of the building where we'd gathered. They didn't rush him. Rather they seemed to want to protect him. They nuzzled against him and escorted him to the sleigh. Because Johnny was blind, his other senses worked overtime. Touching them, petting them, Johnny found strength. Hearing their hoofs pawing the snow, Johnny understood their poise, their grandeur and worth. That understanding of worth translated to Johnny feeling worth and value in his life. He accepted the fact the couple would not be adopting him. He realized that despite the disappointment, his life still had value. That realization came from the reindeer. That is why I feel those reindeer were Santa's reindeer."

"When Santa stopped here on that Christmas Eve before you and your fellow orphans gathered in the woods for a celebration, we had a long talk about Johnny. The young lad had written Santa and told him how his adoption had been called off. Like everyone else, Santa's heart was broken. Instead of toys or games, he felt what Johnny needed most was the compassion and strength of his reindeer. Santa asked that I prepare the herd for a journey to where Johnny would be. I was there, Sophie. I watched the reindeer envelop Johnny. I saw the young boy's reaction. You are a believer, Sophie. You sensed they were Santa's reindeer. And now I will answer your questions."

Walking over toward the tree, Thomas picked up the satchel. He motioned for Steve to join him. Sitting down together as stars sparkled outside under the moonlight, Thomas offered Sophie peace of mind and a surprise she never could have imagined.

"Ironically, Santa had received a letter from Lily about eight months ago explaining she had a sister named Sophie living somewhere in

America and would he please find her. The background you offered in your recent letter mirrored what Lily had described in her letter. Santa put the pieces of the puzzle together and concluded you two were the sisters involved. Lily revealed to Santa she was quite ill. Her fear was that old box full of photos would never reach you because of family members adamant you never be accepted into the fold. So Lily asked Santa to take the old box with its gold clasp. She felt if Santa had possession of the box it would be delivered to you should he locate your whereabouts. So that is what Santa Claus did. He made a special trip in the darkness of a summer night to secure that box in hopes of finding you."

"Why didn't he deliver it to me?"

"Santa just recently learned of your location through your letter. He was overjoyed when realizing you'd be spending Christmas here. When he was told the reason why and that the double wedding would be taking place in this magnificent setting, he knew exactly where to put the box."

"What's so special about this barn, Thomas?"

"This barn, Miss Sophie, is used to carry on tradition. A solemn ceremony is held over by that towering pine—next to that sleigh with the satchel—whenever a new reindeer keeper begins his duties. That sleigh was the first sleigh to go around the world on the first Christmas Eve. And this satchel was Santa's first satchel used to spread the magic of Christmas."

Thomas explained the importance of the sleighs lined up out back and the heartfelt regard Santa showed for Sophie and her sister by placing the old worn box inside that satchel.

"Santa was overwhelmed by your letters. There is nothing more important to Santa than family. For you two to be separated by family ignorance warranted his deepest respect. To Santa, that meant placing the box inside a satchel that represented joy—wonder—and love of family."

"How did Santa know the satchel would be found?"

"Santa believed, Miss Sophie. And he had faith you'd recognize the box once you saw it again. Childhood memories good and bad are first memories. Others are not as vivid as we grow. By leaving it where he did, Santa added even more meaning to a gift from one sister to another."

"Sadly, that box and the photos are all I have of Lily, of a sister I will never know."

Thomas went back to the tree and placed the satchel in the sleigh. Nodding to Edmund, who was coming in from outside, Thomas rejoined Henry and Sophie and asked if they'd stand by his side.

"Santa has recognized you, Henry for the goodness you gave to others. Sophie, Santa wants you to know he hasn't overlooked your good deeds."

"I never asked to be recognized. Any good I may have done was genuine."

"Santa understands the good offered has to be genuine or else it lacks meaning. It is because of your spirit of good will that Santa has sent you a gift."

Henry took hold of Sophie's hand. He felt a miracle was about to take place in that barn in the woods.

"Edmund," spoke Thomas, "Proceed."

While Edmund unhinged the back door, Thomas told Sophie Santa had found more photos of her family.

"But the photos are not in an old box, Sophie. They are being delivered to you by Lily's son, Julian."

Edmund pushed the door open. As snow swirled about and stars glistened, in stepped a distinguished-looking man with dark hair that had a bit of a wave. Sophie could tell his eyes were a deep brown, like hers. That's all she noticed. She moved toward him as fast as she could with her cane in one hand and Henry on her other side and tears rolling down her cheeks.

"Oh my! Oh my boy. My boy!"

"Aunt Sophie! My aunt Sophie!"

That's all they could utter before scooping each other up in an embrace decades in the making. Henry stepped back, crying so hard he could barely catch his breath. Hearing Sophie referred to as Aunt Sophie was an answer to a prayer. All he ever wanted was for Sophie to find peace when it came to her family. Looking at the two wrapped up in emotion, Henry knew his prayer had been answered.

Chapter Twenty-Seven

THE SCENE UNFOLDING IN FRONT OF a tree decorated in glass bulbs straight from the North Pole could have been written for one of those favorite TV Christmas movies watched year after year. Sophie with her cane and hair pulled up in a bun, and Julian, her tall, dark, and handsome nephew—dressed in a long wool coat with leather gloves and a slight hint of a beard—were so overjoyed to be reunited that they couldn't let go of each other even as others welcomed him. Both took deep breaths. Both stood staring at each other. Tears never stopped.

"Welcome, Mr. Julian! Welcome," said Thomas with a wink, introducing himself and the others.

Holding on to her nephew's hand and glancing over at Henry, Sophie explained how precious the moment was to her.

"I search for words. There are none. I remember the euphoria I felt when Benny walked into the back room of my fabric shop, back into my life. That same feeling came over me when Henry walked into Benny's living room, back into my life. Both were returning. When that barn door opened and this handsome lad walked in and called me Aunt Sophie, I heard the heavens sing. Julian was not returning. He was stepping in to my life. I will never get to know my dear sister. God has given me the gift of getting to know her through her son, my dear, dear nephew, Julian."

Again, the tears were falling like the snowflakes brushing against the windowpanes. Adjusting his coat and then his sweater, it was Julian's turn to speak. In a voice strong and sure and in an accent mirroring what Sophie remembered of her father's, Julian thanked everyone for the welcome. Then he took it to a more personal level.

"When my mother realized she was dying, she made me promise I would find you, Aunt Sophie. Thanks to Thomas and his special friend—as explained to me over the phone—this reunion is taking place. What happened to separate you and your sister is inexcusable. Because of ignorance, Aunt Sophie, you and my mother were kept apart. We can't make up for time lost, but I vow to you and to my mother's memory this evening is but a beginning."

Julian reached into a back pocket. As the wind moved snow about the fields, Julian pulled out a small photo from his wallet. He showed it to Sophie. "I see my mother in you, the high cheek bones, shape of the nose, mannerisms. I hear my mother in the tone of your voice, Aunt Sophie. Although you lived apart, find comfort in the fact you were so much alike."

It was ironic that this reunion was happening on New Year's Eve with its atmosphere of celebration. Thomas hurried about with a big grin. Steve stood back while Henry and Sophie shared time with Julian. When there was a moment, Steve went over and introduced himself.

"Welcome, Julian. I'm Steve. It's a pleasure meeting you."

"Thank you, Steve. Thomas told me this amazing place is yours."

"My wife was given all of it as a gift."

"Abbey, right?"

"Yes, Abbey."

Steve changed the subject. There was not enough time to tell the whole story and it wasn't the place to do so.

"While I've only known Sophie for a few days, the joy you've brought her is apparent."

"When I was growing up my mother would talk about Sophie in whispers. She'd show me photos she kept hidden under her mattress. The older I became the more repulsed I was by what my family had done. I have three daughters. I can't imagine deliberately separating them."

"What did your daughters say about Sophie being found?"

"All three thought of their grandmother and how sad it was she'd never get to know her only sister. If I wasn't tied up with business, my daughter Charlotte would be here."

"She wanted to come?"

"She did, but it's been a marathon ever since Thomas called to say his friend had found Sophie. I happened to be coming this way, heading to a trade show in Florida. But I would have been here regardless."

"What line of work are you in?"

"I own a tech firm. I surround myself with a savvy team of young tech minds."

"I understand what you're saying. I owned a lumberyard. My oldest son was responsible for getting the business visible on the web."

"I think customer service can get lost in social media. That's why I like trade shows. It's about meeting people."

"You're not driving all the way, are you?"

"No, not this time of the year. I'm catching a flight in the city."

" Its smart business, Julian, putting a face to your brand. Just like our friend Thomas."

"Talking about me, Mr. Steve?"

"I was saying to Julian how important it is to do a good job no matter what it is you do. No one does that better than you."

"I'm a prime example of your doing a good job, Thomas. If not for you, I wouldn't be here."

Hearing Sophie calling him, Julian excused himself."

Staying by Thomas, Steve remarked, "I have a feeling you and your friend have been busy."

"That we have, Mr. Steve. Once the connection was made between the letters, the process to bring Sophie and Julian together began."

"So Santa met Julian?"

"No. They've never met. Lily explained how close she and Julian were when Santa stopped for the box. When he learned Sophie would be here for the wedding, I contacted Julian. He has no inkling of Santa Claus, if you know what I mean, Mr. Steve. Julian was most gracious on the phone. He went out of his way to be here if only for a few hours."

"What a puzzle to put together! How did Julian get to this barn? And whatever inspired Henry and Sophie to get in that sleigh and trust the horses would get them here by flying them through the night?"

"Julian and I set a time when he would arrive at your place. I told him where we would be. I explained the barn was only accessible by sleigh so I would have my son meet him and bring him here. As far as what inspired Henry and Sophie, I sense belief and faith joined as one and filled Henry's heart at that specific moment on this earth. Not just anyone would have been in tune with what the heavens were sending over fields and valleys and though the pine and cedar. But Henry heard it. Henry reacted. Santa knew he would."

Steve didn't need to hear any more explanation. He believed what Thomas was saying. If one is in tune, one can hear the whispering wind singing its song just for them.

Realizing Julian's time was limited, Thomas asked everyone to follow him.

"How did you pull this off?" asked Steve as Thomas escorted everyone into the back room where he'd covered a table in a familiar lace tablecloth. Placed on top were trays of gourmet meats and cheeses, plus breads and casseroles right out of the oven, along with delectable desserts and piping hot apple cider filling a crock pot topped with lemon and orange slices. Aromas of maple syrup and cinnamon drifted up to the rafters and back.

"Eric and his staff were most helpful. Despite it being New Year's Eve, Eric made this gathering a priority. When we are finished, the staff will come back and bring whatever remains to the farmhouse."

"I had no clue this was going on."

"Sometimes a surprise turns out to be a good thing, Mr. Steve."

"Since we first met, Thomas, life has been a constant surprise!"

With holiday plates and vintage mugs being filled and refilled, the atmosphere was one of elation.

Watching Julian with Sophie, it was hard to believe they'd just met. That was her doing. Sophie made Julian feel welcome. Going through the photos together, Sophie made certain he understood she held no hard feelings for what had happened so long ago.

"Life throws everyone curves," she explained. "You have to make the best of it."

"You've done that and more, Aunt Sophie. My mother showed me these photos many times. She never got over the two of you being separated."

Julian explained who was in each one. When it came to a rather large photo, there was no explanation needed.

"While I have a few photos of our mother, I've never seen her so young. Her skin is flawless—her smile so warm."

"That's you she's holding, Aunt Sophie. Mother told me you were three weeks old."

It was hard for Sophie to focus through the tears. So she concentrated on what she knew best to settle her down.

"The fabric—I think that's a white batiste. I'm certain it is. The way the blouse drapes down off her shoulders shows how lightweight it was. Perfect for such a delicate garment trimmed in Victorian lace. And would you look at me—all dressed up in what I'd say was hand-crocheted lace."

"Your mother made the outfit, Aunt Sophie. I understand she knitted that blanket in the photo as well."

Taking an even closer look, Sophie noted the craftsmanship of her mother's work. Sophie imagined those hands looping the yarn from one needle to the next. She could feel the warmth of the yarn—smell the sweet scent of the African Violets sitting behind them near the window.

"Mama was so beautiful," whispered Sophie.

It was Thomas who interrupted the moment.

"Pardon me, Miss Sophie. But I do think it is time for you to leave, Mr. Julian. You have a long way yet to go."

Pausing, Sophie switched her focus to her nephew.

"Thomas is right, Julian I don't want you to be in a rush."

Sophie's understanding made it easier for Julian to say goodbye.

"I love you, Aunt Sophie. I felt my mother beside us tonight. I will call you from Florida."

"You have brought a joy into my life I can't explain, Julian. Be safe and know that I love you."

With Edmund waiting, Julian shook Henry's hand. There were no words exchanged. A bear hug from Henry was enough.

"I enjoyed our conversation, although brief, Steve."

"It was a pleasure, Julian. I have a feeling we will be seeing each other again."

By the time Julian made it to the door, Thomas was standing by his son.

"Please thank your friend for making this night happen, Thomas. I'll never be able to repay him."

"You have repaid him by coming, by giving Sophie your heart, Mr. Julian. That is a priceless gift indeed."

In an instant, Edmund and Julian went out the door. Shortly after that Henry and Sophie were on their way as well. Steve and Thomas tried to get them to wait until morning, but they wanted to get back home.

"So much has happened. I feel a drive among the stars is the best way to travel tonight," Sophie had explained

Surrounded by trees holding lanterns, Thomas and Steve watched as Henry began maneuvering his sleigh through the woods. Once the sleigh was out of sight, they waited. It wasn't long before they could see the sleigh heading up into the night and then straight north. It certainly had been a New Year's Eve like no other.

Chapter Twenty-Eight

BACK INSIDE THE BARN, THOMAS AND Steve began cleaning up. Fancy dishes were covered in foil. Casserole tops were found and trays cleared. Mugs and plates were put in boxes.

"Miss Abbey's lace tablecloth added the perfect touch. I hope you didn't mind my using it again, Mr. Steve,"

"I was happy you did. Sophie noticed."

"Being a person of detail, Miss Sophie would."

"The look on her face when the barn door opened and Julian walked in was like that of a child on Christmas morning."

"Exactly, Mr. Steve. Miss Sophie exemplifies awe and wonder."

Blowing out the candles, the two put everything they had ready to go near the door. When Edmund returned, he and two of Eric's staff put the boxes in the sleigh and journeyed back again to the farmhouse.

"Edmund will be back shortly, Mr. Steve. Let us sit by the tree. It is getting late. My plan is to leave after stopping to see Greta early in the morning."

Steve knew what that meant. It was time to discuss Steve's choice as to who would follow at some point as the reindeer keeper's helper. And then they would say goodbye.

With the moon flickering through the stained-glass windows and the wind whispering about the trees, the two sat for one last time in designated roles other than good friends.

"I understand why believing is even more important as we grow older."

"It's hard to do when adulthood is involved , Mr. Steve."

"That was the deciding point."

"Please explain."

"I was down to three choices, Greta, Henry, and Meg. You once told me neither age nor distance matter. That was important to know since the three offer a vast diversity in qualifications."

"The most important qualification is what lies within that person's heart. The three are all fine choices. How did you come to your conclusion?"

"One night I woke up from a sound sleep. Something was telling me to read the letter Abbey had left with you to give to me. When I did, my choice became clear. I feel Greta has the potential. But youthful potential must be tested.

"Life is the test, Mr. Steve."

"For sure. So that left me with Henry and Meg. Both have been tested. But when I read Abbey's words, one stood out."

Reaching inside a back pocket, Steve added, "I don't know why I bothered to bring the letter with me. I know it word for word."

"It brings you reassurance, Mr. Steve."

"All the time."

Steve read a few of Abbey's words in the place she considered her church in the woods. *It can never destroy my love for you.*

"Those words made me think of Henry and his undying love of Sophie and loyalty to Helen and the happiness he gave to those without families. He did that out of compassion. He's never faltered. He's never given up. Henry finds joy in the little things and believes in that childhood wonder. Did I consider his age? Did I think of the distance between here and there? For an instant I did. But in the end, none of that matters. Will he live to replace me? That is left to fate, left to the winds and snowfalls and wisdom of others to determine. Within

Henry lies a dreamer, a believer. And because of that, Henry is my choice, Thomas."

"I applaud your decision, Mr. Steve. I'm often dismayed by the disregard shown the elderly. Their wisdom should be respected. When you asked me why Santa had insisted we deliver that sleigh to Henry, a part of me thought Santa sensed you'd choose Henry. That sleigh will afford him quick access to this place, as evident tonight."

"I seriously considered Meg. She continues to be a great help to me. Without her, I don't know how I would have carried on after losing Abbey. I feel her day will come. But for now, this is Henry's time to be the reindeer keeper's helper."

The barn door opening and Edmund walking in shifted the conversation.

"Edmund, I am taking Mr. Steve home. When I return, we can close down the barn for tonight."

It was as if the heavens had ordered the moon and stars and glittering snowflakes to be in harmony for the two friends riding through the woods and over the fields of snow back to the farmhouse. They didn't speak. They left that up to nature's backdrop.

"Need help with anything, Thomas?" asked Steve as the horses came to a halt by the back steps.

Steve knew the answer. He knew he was the one in need of help saying goodbye to the little man who'd never wavered in his loyalty to both he and Abbey.

"Thanks to your assistance, everything is in order, Mr. Steve. You've remained steadfast. Abbey knew you would."

"I've been blessed by your friendship. That friendship will stay with me forever."

"Before I go, Mr. Steve, I must repeat what I've said to you before. Moving on is the natural thing to do. Life is change. Putting it bluntly, Mr. Steve, Susan is your next step. Miss Abbey would tell you the same. Now I must go spend time with the reindeer keeper. Please remember I will not be far away."

"I value your wisdom, Thomas, and your honesty."

Jumping down off the sleigh, Steve headed toward home but

stopped. Turning around as the horses snorted and that late night train chugged down tracks far away, he added, "Take good care of Dancer, Thomas."

"That's exactly what Abbey asked of me, Mr. Steve, when we said good bye!"

"Why am I not surprised?"

Standing on the steps of the old farmhouse, he watched as Thomas disappeared into the night. So many memories went dashing along with that sleigh and with a friendship he'd cherish forever. Funny how we connect with certain people in ways that make us better—make us whole. That type of friend is a rare find indeed. Once back inside, Steve found a note waiting for him on the kitchen table. It was from Sammy.

"Dad, Susan called to wish you a Happy New Year."

Grabbing the note, he went upstairs. Once settled in bed with those glittering stars still shining and the moon enhancing the falling snow-flakes, Steve called Susan. They talked into the wee hours of the morning.

Chapter Twenty-Nine

With Edmund in his new role for a little over a month, Steve was starting to feel things were settling in. He'd talked to Thomas more than once about clearing an area near the front of the barn for a wood shop. It wasn't being used for anything in particular. It was far enough away from the animals that their routine would not be disturbed.

"When I use my power tools, I'll keep the door closed," Steve had explained. "Nothing could get through that solid piece of white oak."

"That's the way this barn was built, Mr. Steve," was Thomas's reply.

Before he'd sold the lumberyard, Steve brought lots of materials home. Over Christmas, Ben told Steve he was busier than ever since retiring.

"When Ellie and I went on road trips though New Hampshire, I'd collect old things with the intention of restoring them once I had the time. I'm in the middle of bringing that old Hoosier cabinet back to life. It's a beauty—has the flour bin, the bread drawer with the metal lid. I love the history of such a piece. My father's always full of stories about whatever it is I'm working on."

While Ben liked restoring old things, Steve planned to build new things. Once he had the space the way he wanted it, Steve was ready to get started. The timing was perfect. Meg and the kids were away for a week. She almost canceled the visit to her mother's, but a remark Greta made one night at supper when talking to Eric convinced Meg it was the right thing to do.

"Are you excited to meet your grandmother?" he'd asked.

"I can't wait. I want to tell my new grandma about Miracle and my other grandma in heaven."

If for no other reason than to give her children the opportunity to have a grandmother in their lives, Meg packed them up, and off they went.

"I don't know what's going to happen," she'd told Eric when saying goodbye at the airport. "But I have to try."

With Steve and Eric being the only ones home and Eric working late at the restaurant, Steve found himself with idle time. He had the idea of making a bookcase. It'd be for Meg. She still had books stacked high in boxes since moving from New York. After the rush of the holidays, Steve thought getting back to creating with his hands would be the perfect way to recoup. It felt good when working alongside Thomas building the addition, but he hadn't undertaken any projects on his own since losing Abbey. He couldn't. He'd get an idea, start to plan it out, and then quit. This time he was determined. He had the space with all his tools, a drawing table, plenty of wood, and anything else he might need. The only problem was that same problem as before: he couldn't concentrate on it long enough to even start. A phone call from a stranger early one morning took Steve's mind off his problem. At first, he thought it was one of those quick survey calls because of the questions being asked. He almost hung up until questions turned to a familiar name.

"I didn't mean to sound odd, Steve. I had to make sure I'd called the right person. I'm part of an artist's guild in Portland. Susan is being honored for her work this coming Saturday. She has mentioned you a few times since getting back here. I can't explain it, but something told me I had to call and let you know about the event. If you think you'd be interested in surprising her, I'd be happy to email you information and directions."

Steve didn't know what to say. It was as if this stranger had sensed he'd been thinking of Susan but couldn't take that next step Thomas mentioned again when saying goodbye. If Steve was honest with himself, he'd admit Susan was the reason he found himself restless. She'd gotten to him. From the moment they started talking at the reunion, he was interested in her.

Steve gave the woman on the phone his email address and thanked her for calling. Even before he hung up, Steve was figuring out how soon he could get on the road. His first move was dialing Ben's number. The phone only rang once, and Ben was at the other end, surprised and pleased to hear from Steve.

"Great to hear you're coming this way. Plan on an overnight with us. Then we'll have time to catch up and I can show you my workshop. I'll make sure my parents join us for dinner."

When Steve asked how far he was from Portland, Ben knew why.

"You've changed your mind about visiting Susan?"

"Yes I have."

"A road trip is a great way to clear the mind. I told you how Ellie and I still go whenever we can. We'll talk more when you get here. See you in a few days."

After touching base with Ben, Steve decided to email Eric and fill him in. That wasn't an easy thing to do. While waiting for the computer to load, so many memories went flashing through his mind and they all included Abbey. Getting up out of his chair, Steve poured himself a second cup of coffee. The old house was quiet. Looking out the back door, he noticed a flutter of wings at one of the bird feeders. Before Greta left she'd filled them with sunflower seeds. It was the seeds causing the commotion. They'd attracted the Snow Buntings—Abbey's favorites. Steve hadn't seen them around in quite a while. Watching the birds, he remembered Abbey saying how the little birds brought her peace of mind. She couldn't explain why. It was something about them—so innocent— so beautiful. Sitting back down at the table, Steve emailed his oldest son, telling him he was driving to Maine to see Susan.

Chapter Thirty

By Friday, Steve was on the road with Google maps and a thermos of coffee. The event was to take place the following evening at a hotel offering a spectacular view of the ocean. He'd checked the forecast. There was only a slight chance of snow near Portland starting Saturday afternoon. It didn't matter. Once Steve made his decision to go, nothing could have stopped him.

Steve found the old stone home surrounded by a stone wall almost buried in snow just as Ben described. Parking next to the carriage house, Steve went inside to find Ben stripping old paint off the Hoosier cabinet he'd mentioned.

"You weren't kidding. That piece is a gem."

"It dates back to 1910. It's in amazing shape."

The two men shook hands. After asking about his trip, Ben pulled out a stool. "Have a seat in my office. We can talk while I finish this door. Ellie has dinner cooking. We're pleased you'll be staying the night."

As Ben applied a few more coats of guck, Steve started talking. He felt at ease with Ben. They were close in age. It was like having the brother he never had. Growing up the middle child, Steve had no one to talk to. His sisters were always fighting.

"Tell me about the award Susan is receiving."

"I was told she's being recognized by her peers for her exceptional talent and achievements."

"Does she know you will be there?"

"No. The person who called suggested I surprise her."

"Well, you surprised us!"

As Ben kept working, Steve looked around.

"You said you collected a few things on your road trips. I see more than a few!"

"Everything has a story. My problem is I want to make sure they're all told."

"This cutter must be your father's."

"Of all his sleighs and cutters, it's his favorite. He and my mother rode in this cutter the day he asked her to marry him. He's sentimental like that."

"A sentimental poet. There's nothing wrong with that."

"That's my dad. A sentimental poet with a heavy foot."

"Looks like he had a fender-bender in his favorite cutter."

"He didn't take a wide enough turn and found himself in a thicket. I have to glue the boards back together and replace the runners. Those are the originals. I looked them up. They're what is called Barrel Stave runners. Almost impossible to find these days so I'm planning on making a pair of curved ski runners."

"What's involved?"

"It's a process of gluing together several thin strips of wood—then using lots of clamps and glue. Dad won't be back in this cutter until next season."

"I can see Henry out in the fields, speeding along."

"That's exactly what happened. My mother was upset. She was afraid of what could have happened to him—out there all alone."

"I guess I never paid attention to the difference between a sleigh and a cutter. Now I can see how much smaller a cutter is in comparison to a sleigh."

"That's the main difference. It's perfect for one or two and that's about it."

"Interesting," said Steve, looking at the cutter from all angles.

Dinner was served in grand style with a fire in the fireplace and a toast to their guest. It was obvious how pleased Henry was that Steve was on his way to see Susan.

"You can't stay in the shadows. You have to declare to Susan and the universe how you feel."

"Maybe you could write Steve some poetry. That always works on me." Sophie laughed.

"I need all the help I can get. I'm not good at this. I can't figure out how some people go from being with one and then another and sometimes another with not much time between them."

"We each have different needs. When I married Helen, it was for the companionship. Working a farm takes an understanding partner and that was Helen."

"Lives come in stages," said Sophie. "Trouble is we never know when one might end."

Ben helped Ellie serve dessert in the front room. They sat and talked till close to midnight.

Steve got back on the road by midmorning. Once close to the bridge in Portsmouth, he didn't have far to go. Trouble was, it'd snowed most of the night. It wasn't letting up. It wasn't supposed to be snowing yet according to sources he'd checked and rechecked. With traffic hardly moving, Steve began doubting his decision to make the trip in the first place. Was this a sign to turn around and go back home? If so, he wasn't able to turn around so he kept going. If he went back home, he'd only be thinking of Susan.

He still would have arrived when planned if it hadn't been for an accident. Traffic came to a halt. Even after the highway was cleared, conditions were so bad that everyone slowed to a crawl. Steve wished he had a horse and sleigh.

When he finally made it to the hotel, Steve had no time to waste. He noted a sign inside the lobby giving those attending the art guild's event directions to where the affair would be taking place. By the looks of the dress of a few coming in behind him, Steve was certain they were there for the occasion. He hurried to his room.

If he'd had the time, Steve would have relaxed and enjoyed the view of the harbor. Instead, he took a quick shower, dressed, and went back downstairs. By then the room was crowded with people. He could see the head table. To the left, pieces of Susan's artwork were on display. A podium was to the right. His thought was to sit near the door to surprise Susan when she came in but most of the tables had names at every place setting.

It turned out Steve was the one surprised. As he was making his way through the crowd, he happened to look over as Susan was entering the room. She was stunning. Dressed in an off-the-shoulder black dress with simple lines and her hair left to fall naturally, Susan caught everyone's attention. They all stood and clapped.

Grabbing Steve's attention even more was the fact Susan was not alone. She was on the arm of a man dressed in a fine suit. Susan looked like a natural by his side—smiling—making quick conversation with those who stopped them. Hugging some—joking with others, Steve was surprised at the Susan he was watching. It was a totally different person than the Susan he had a hard time saying goodbye to as snow fell and a little ceramic tree added to the moment.

Trying to get a closer look while remaining obscure, Steve considered the man by her side to be of the artsy type. But then he was judging the man by his purple jacquard tie and hint of a beard. Maybe the guy's on the guild's board. Maybe he's an old friend. Maybe he's Susan's relative or maybe he's her new interest while in Maine. So many maybes went through Steve's mind as he watched the two of them work the crowd. Susan was at ease surrounded by those dressed in glitter and brand names. Steve heard her say how surprised she'd been when learning the evening was in her honor.

Moving to the back of the room, Steve continued watching. When the man in the artsy tie pulled Susan close and kissed her as they were about to sit down, Steve reached his limit. He'd had enough. Heading to the door, Steve turned around and looked back at her one last time. Then he left the room.

Asking the desk clerk where he might get a good meal and a cold beer, Steve exited the hotel and went nearby to enjoy some fine Maine seafood. When back in his room, he sat in front of the window and took in the harbor. Sitting there, Steve concluded the dating thing wasn't for him. He had no interest in pursuing someone in a cat-and-mouse style game. If it didn't happen on its own, Steve was not going to play. He never had to play games with Abbey. They were simply meant to be. That's how he decided to leave it with Susan. If they were meant to be, then it would happen. He would know if and when he should make a move. Steve felt like a misfit with those still gathered in that ballroom downstairs. It was the moon showing up off in the distance that brought him back to his senses—realizing he felt like a misfit because he was a misfit. He wasn't about glitter and champagne. That moon connected him with woods and pastures—old barns and a farmhouse he called home. He'd get a good night's sleep and head back to that place in the morning.

The next day at seven am, Steve was on his way with a coffee in hand, anticipating the rolling fields, the barn with those reindeer, and his waiting workspace.

Chapter Thirty-One

ONE GOOD THING STEVE GAINED FROM his road trip was an idea for a project. This time he was excited to get it started. This time he knew he would—deciding whatever might or might not happen with Susan was out of his hands. They still talked on the phone. He never let on he'd been in the ballroom that Saturday night.

Steve fell into his project. Whenever Greta came to the barn, he made sure the door was secure. He had his reasons.

"What are you building, Grandpa?" she'd ask over and over.

"I can't tell. It's a surprise."

Although she would turn seven in July, Greta still believed in Santa Claus. Considering the surroundings and the goodness in her heart, she'd probably believe forever.

One evening in early March, when the kids were sleeping, Meg and Eric were sitting in the front room with a fire in the fireplace. Steve was in his chair. Out of the blue, Meg started talking about her visit with her mother. She'd talked about it when returning but needed time to mull it over before going into detail.

"I found my mother to be a quiet, gracious woman. I went from calling her Elizabeth to Mom in a matter of minutes. She opened her arms and heart to us, apologizing repeatedly for the years we'd wasted.

I'd remind her I too was responsible for the time we'd lost. I enjoyed her stories of being a secretary to a law firm."

"Ironic your mom worked for a law firm, Meg, when you yourself are a lawyer."

"I found that ironic too, Steve. We both did. She knows her stuff. It led to our having some interesting conversations."

"Greta told me her grandmother makes the best popcorn," laughed Eric.

"Mom told me her trick. She sprinkles a bit of cinnamon on top. With the butter, it melts into the popcorn, honey."

"I'll have to try that at the restaurant. People love new munchies."

"Mom fell in love with Greta and Bobby. She'd rock Bobby back to sleep the few times he woke during the night. Greta talked her into a knitting project for her dolls. Greta also told her grandmother about Abbey and Miracle. I could tell Greta felt comfortable with her. She even told Mom about leaving the apples and oranges out for the wild horses and how she'd fed them by hand. Mom was speechless."

"I can hear Greta telling the story. That would leave anyone speechless," laughed Steve.

"When we were at the airport, Greta invited her for Christmas."

"What was your mother's response?" asked Eric.

"She accepted."

"Christmas is taking shape again. Truth is, Christmas is never far away."

"You're right, Dad. The older I get, the more I realize Christmas is much more than a day. It's a state of mind."

"I'm already thinking what it will be like to have my mother here on Christmas Eve and when the kids open their gifts Christmas morning."

"It will be here with a blink of an eye," said Steve, thinking of Thomas.

And Steve was right. Time flew. Steve and Susan kept meeting for coffee. They'd had dinner together but that was it. Whenever she'd asked him to stay, he'd make up an excuse and then leave, wishing he'd stayed the night. He still hadn't been able to tell her he was in that ballroom when she walked in looking beautiful and confident. He wanted to ask about the artsy man in the tie but held back. He wanted to hold her and tell her how he felt, but he didn't.

When they all went to Maggie and Teddy's May reception in New York and Sammy and Cate's reception in LA in October, Steve wanted to ask Susan to go with him, but he didn't. He remained stubborn while wishing for some sort of a sign or something that in some way would move him—move them forward. Steve avoided talking to Henry about Susan. He knew what the old man would say. He'd said it over and over again: "You have to declare to Susan and the universe how you feel."

When Christmas rolled around, Steve kept his attention on the project he'd about completed. But deep down, his heart was with the artist down Route 93 in a Quaker-style home with a cranberry door.

Chapter Thirty-Two

SHADES OF PINKS AND PURPLES SPREAD across the horizon. With the sun waking up, those streaks turned fields of snow into a shimmering palette. To those who'd be gathering later when the moon came out and the barn and reindeer welcomed old friends back once more, colorful crystals would again be part of the wonder of Christmas Eve. While Eric added fresh blueberries to pancake batter, Meg picked up items left around from the night before. With her mother still sleeping, she tip-toed around the kitchen.

"I want this Christmas to be perfect. I have a feeling my mother hasn't celebrated the holidays in years."

"I thought she celebrated with your brother."

"I don't think she put much effort into it. Reminds me of when we lived in New York and I was consumed with power. Christmas was an inconvenience."

"I was as consumed as you were. Wall Street sucked me in. We were both lost to the system."

"We're lucky aren't we?"

"In so many ways."

"Are you happy, Eric?"

"Happy?" Going over to Meg, Eric wrapped his arms around her. "You have defined happiness in a way I never thought possible."

"Think some of those people still playing the game are happy?"

"People define happiness in different ways, Meg."

"I used to think it was all about making the kill, making more money. Now I find happiness in my garden, my children, and your arms."

"We are so lucky, Meg. So very lucky."

A slight breeze moving snow over fields and passing by windows decorated with tin snowmen added to the moment as did scents from a tree in the front room. They'd found the blue spruce in the back woods and brought it home on a toboggan hitched to a sleigh. Cinnamon sprinkled over cutout cookies made by a grandmother and granddaughter getting to know each other mingled with aromas of bayberry candles and molasses mixed with flour and sugar ready to be turned into dough for more cookies once this day before Christmas got underway.

"I loved how my mother took to you yesterday even after a long trip. That was her first time on a plane in years."

"She told me she read a book all the way."

"In her living room, there are shelves full of books."

"Last night when you and Greta were in the kitchen getting the dessert ready to be served, your mother told me she'd kept a photo of you on her bed stand and every night she'd say a prayer you would one day reach out to her. Dad told her how he keeps Mom's letter in his night stand."

"They hit if off the minute they met."

"It was as if they were old friends. Dad promised her a sleigh ride into the woods today."

"And Greta has those cookies she wants to bake and a knitting lesson is planned. Mom expressed interest in going to the cemetery in the morning if you don't mind. I've talked so much about Abbey that she wants to pay her respects—thank her for opening my heart."

"I'm sure it's fine. I'm hoping Dad gets out of his funk by then."

"Funk?"

She was confused. Meg hadn't noticed any difference in Steve but then she'd been absorbed in her mother visiting and getting ready for Christmas.

"I've been so distracted by everything else that I haven't paid that much attention. Do you think he's feeling well?"

"I can read his every mood. Something is off and it's not his health. He'd say so if that was the problem."

"Has he mentioned Susan lately?"

"Not much. I never thought Susan would be the reason."

"When you think about it, Eric, they haven't budged from where they were last year at this time. But maybe that's how they want it. Or maybe your father is stuck. Maybe he doesn't know what to do—how to make a move."

"That's an interesting perspective, honey. Maybe it is Susan who's under his skin."

Folding a touch of nutmeg into the mix, Eric remembered a conversation he'd had with Sammy earlier in the week. He was supposed to keep it a secret. But he couldn't stop from sharing it with Meg.

"You have to act surprised when Greta opens Sammy and Cate's gift," he whispered, as if a certain little girl might hear what he was saying.

"Tell me what it is!"

"It's a rough video of the documentary."

"That's so exciting !"

"Sammy wanted to surprise everyone but I had to tell you. He was awarded funding through Sundance. *Miracle and the Little Girl in the Pink Snowsuit*" is in the works!"

"Oh how wonderful! We'll have to take our little cowgirl to see it. Wonder if Mom would like to fly to Utah?"

"Utah! I haven't been here twenty-four hours and you're shipping me out?"

The hugging started all over again in the kitchen of the old farmhouse. Over a cup of coffee, Eric filled Meg's mother in on how the documentary came about. As he was finishing the story, Greta came down the backstairs. Bobby was close behind. When Steve came in from the barn, they sat down for breakfast. The day was beginning.

Everyone was anticipating Sammy and Cate arriving. Meg and her mom would help Greta and Bobby ready their stockings. Eric's staff would check to see when he'd like dinner to arrive.

"I'd love that kind of service. I wish I lived closer."

"Maybe you should think about that," said Meg.

"Please. Please move by me, Grandma. We could have fun."

"I can tell you from personal experience, Elizabeth," said Steve, "Greta and Bobby will see to it that you are never bored."

"I've noticed signs in the library announcing knitting groups and sometimes the library needs volunteers," added Meg.

"There's so much to consider. I'd have to sell my home first."

"Your home is lovely. It needs nothing. The way the market is, you wouldn't have a problem finding a buyer."

A knock at the door interrupted the conversation just as Elizabeth said she would seriously consider the suggestion.

"Good morning, Edmund. Come in. Would you like a pancake? Cup of coffee?"

"No thank you, Mr. Steve."

"You're just like your father."

After meeting Elizabeth, Edmund continued. "You mentioned you would like to go to the woods this afternoon, Mr. Steve. I have some duties I must complete. I could have the team ready to go by three o'clock. Would that be too late?"

"Perfect! By that time Sammy will be here, and I know cookies are on the agenda so three o'clock will work. We'll meet you at the barn. I'd like to give Elizabeth a tour of the place."

After the kitchen was cleaned up, Eric ran to the restaurant for a little while. More presents were put under the tree. Greta and Bobby stayed in their pajamas as dough was rolled out on the counter. Flour was everywhere.

"Look, Grandma! It's snowing," Greta laughed, shaking flour off her fingers.

"Look outside, Greta. It really is snowing." Elizabeth placed Christmas tree shapes and snowmen shapes and whatever else was being created on a cookie sheet.

"Our snowflakes taste better." Greta rolled up a small ball of dough and ate it.

"I think Steve was right when he told me I'd never be bored."

"I know he was right, Mom."

Once the baking was complete, a platter of molasses cookies sat on the kitchen counter. Soon the house was cleaned up and the kids were dressed. As Greta tried holding small knitting needles, the kitchen door opened. With arms full of gifts, Sammy and Cate entered. They were home again for Christmas.

Chapter Thirty-Three

By the time Eric returned, the house was bustling. Anticipation was increasing as everyone readied for a sleigh ride.

"Don't forget the trunk full of extra scarves and mittens if anyone feels the need for more. Bundle up. It's colder in the woods," said Steve, zipping up his parka.

"Meg gave me some long johns. I haven't worn long johns since skating on the pond where I grew up."

"I didn't know you could skate, Mom."

"I haven't in years."

"There's a pond out back," said Sammy. "We could shovel it and go skating, Elizabeth."

"Let's see how I survive a sleigh ride in the woods first!"

By the time they were dressed and the thermoses were filled, it was a little before three. Eric led the way down to the barn, pulling a wooden sleigh carrying Bobby and Greta. Snow that once clung to branches swirled by this family that had endured so much yet felt so blessed. That's what life's about. Every family's been there.

"Where did you find that little sleigh, Meg? The kids fit in it perfectly."

"Remember I told you about Henry and Sophie? Henry is a master when it comes to sleighs. He sent it to them a few weeks ago."

"Henry looks just like Santa, Grandma. I saw him fly by my window last Christmas Eve."

"Really now? I'd say my granddaughter has a great imagination!"

No one replied. Sometimes it's best that way.

After they reached the barn, Steve held the door while the others went inside.

"I haven't been in a barn in years. The worn wood—the haylofts—the windows—some covered in burlap—all of it is welcoming to one who feels as though she's only been existing. The sweet aroma of hay reminds me of summer fields and patches of wildflowers. It's magnificent. I can't think of a better place to spend Christmas. I can feel Christmas in this barn."

"Edmund, your hard work is apparent."

"Thank you, Mr. Steve. The sleigh is outside. We're ready to go."

"Mind if we take Elizabeth in to see the reindeer?"

"Not at all. The reindeer are brushed and ready, Mr. Steve."

"Ready?" asked Elizabeth.

"Well, it is Christmas Eve, Mom," laughed Meg.

On their way to the reindeer stall, Greta pointed out Miracle's bed of hay.

"Edmund told me we can leave the hay there, Grandma, for as long as I want to. When it was really cold outside I'd cover Miracle with a blanket and he'd go right to sleep."

"Your mommy covers you up with extra blankets when it's cold outside," said Eric.

"Did you cover Mommy, Grandma, when she was cold?"

"In my heart I did, Greta."

It was quiet the rest of the way. The might and wonder of the reindeer turned the mood back to where it had been before a little girl asked a simple question.

"Look, Grandma! See my runt. Edmund lets me brush her just like Thomas did."

"They're all spectacular, Greta. Being among them makes me feel Christmas even more."

Realizing the time, Eric suggested they get going.

With Steve sitting by Edmund and everyone in the back of the sleigh covered in comforters, the horses began their journey. Whizzing over fields and around thickets, they were soon approaching the edge of the woods. Edmund slowed the horses down and took them around birch and maple. Pine trees covered in snow took on an even more lustrous aura as the barn enhanced by lanterns inside and out could be seen.

Elizabeth fell in love with the barn in the woods and its odd collections of things. She heard about the wedding that had taken place a year earlier. She heard so much about Thomas she felt as if she knew him. The glass bulbs decorating a marvelous tree turned Elizabeth speechless, as it had everyone else. They could have stayed longer. But Greta kept reminding them Santa was coming. So was dinner.

A few hours later they were still sitting around the table after feasting on a good old-fashioned turkey dinner with homemade apple and pumpkin pies for dessert. Greta and Bobby weren't interested in pie. They went in the front room and played by the tree. Greta kept peeking out the window. The phone ringing in the kitchen grabbed Steve's attention.

"Merry Christmas to you, too, Henry, and to Sophie and the family. We were thinking of you this afternoon. Meg's mom is visiting. We took her to the barn in the woods."

Henry was happy for Meg. He told Steve they had visitors as well.

"I'm glad to hear Julian and his daughters are there. Sophie must be elated."

Everyone took a turn talking with Henry. Sophie got on the phone, joking that their home was full of French Canadians. Ellie and Ben sent their love.

Eric's staff was back. They took care of everything. While everyone gathered in the front room, the kitchen was back in shape in no time. It wasn't long before Greta and Bobby were in their pajamas and hanging their stockings.

"Before we go upstairs, you have to put your cookies and milk out for Santa," said Meg. "Your letters to Santa are in the top of my desk, Greta."

Everyone watched while the Christmas Eve tradition came together once again. Molasses cookies in all shapes and sizes sat on that same plate used year after year. Next to the cookies sat the letters and glass of milk and of course, sugar for the reindeer. Once Greta and Bobby were upstairs, it wasn't long before everyone else followed. Tomorrow would be a busy day.

Chapter Thirty-Four

THE HOUSE RETURNED TO QUIET. STEVE stayed up, sitting by the fire. So many thoughts, so many feelings, had crossed his mind the last few months. He wanted to tell Susan how he felt but after seeing her in Portland he didn't know what to do. It was all too hard. Going over to the window and looking out, he didn't hear someone approaching.

"Can't sleep?"

Startled, Steve turned around.

"I didn't mean to frighten you."

"I was a million miles away, Eric."

"I thought you might be. You've seemed preoccupied lately. I was wondering if you'd like to talk."

"I'm stuck."

"I don't understand, Dad."

Sitting back down in his chair, Steve spoke in a whisper, shaking his head. "I'm such a fool."

Eric didn't respond. He waited.

"I drove all the way to Portland. I stopped at Ben and Ellie's along the way. Saw Henry and Sophie. Had dinner with them. Stayed the night. They all knew I was on my way to surprise Susan."

"When you got back you never said how it went."

"You never asked."

"It felt strange, Dad."

"I get that. I feel awkward talking to you about another woman."

"Dad," said Eric, pulling a chair close to his father's, "your being with Susan in no way diminishes what you felt for Mom. You don't have to explain a thing. One night after we'd moved her bed onto the porch, Mom told me she prayed you'd fall in love all over again. You seem to be seeking a sign, a whisper, something words can't provide that would be the catalyst pushing you forward. Be open, Dad. I'm here for you anytime you want to talk." Saying good night, Eric started to leave.

"I never spoke to her."

"Never spoke to whom, Dad?"

"Susan. When I went to Portland, I never spoke to her."

Eric sat back down.

"I saw her but we didn't speak. She never knew I was there. I was part of the crowd as she came into the room."

Everything was making sense now.

"What happened? Why didn't you speak?"

"She was with another man."

"Do you know who the guy was?"

"No but I saw him kiss her when they were getting ready to sit down."

"You read too much into something you watched from afar."

"Standing there surrounded by strangers, I felt out of place. I felt . . ."

"You felt what?"

"I felt awkward. I felt, in her eyes, I'd never measure up to the artsy types in that room. That's not me. That's why I feel stuck. I can't figure out what to do. I'm too old to play the game. I've never done that. I don't know the rules. If I knew the rules, I wouldn't play anyway."

"Remember the first Christmas in this farmhouse? Remember the night after we arrived? I was in the kitchen helping Mom with dinner and was amazed to find she'd kept many of the cookbooks I'd collected as a kid."

"I remember that like it was yesterday."

"Remember when you came in to the kitchen? You remarked how it was a sight for sore eyes seeing the two of us cooking together again?"

"Yes. I remember."

"Just before that, before you came in, Mom had told me that no matter the situation I should never feel stuck. She told me once I make a decision, things would fall into place. Her words were all I needed. Her words changed my life around. And Mom's words can do the same for you right now."

"I don't understand what you mean."

"Let me be blunt. Do you love Susan?"

"Susan is beautiful. Talented. Pleasant to be around."

"All adjectives. I asked if you loved her."

With that angel sitting at the top of the tree and letters and cookies waiting for Santa, Steve looked his eldest in the eyes and simply replied, "Yes."

"Then you have to go tell her."

"You were right when you said I'm seeking something words can't provide."

"Then stay vigilant, Dad. That moment will happen. I know it will."

Eric said good night again and went back upstairs. Steve fell sound asleep next to the tree.

CLOSE TO TEN, HE FELT A tugging on his sleeve. Then he heard a whisper. "Grandpa. Grandpa. The snow woke me up."

Half awake, Steve held out his arms. Greta climbed in his lap and told him how pretty it was outside.

"Is it still snowing, honey?"

"Coming down in buckets, Grandpa."

What Greta said stirred a memory. Her words had been his words when Abbey asked one evening when she was so sick if it was snowing. Steve realized at that moment he and Greta were destined to go outside and make snow angels, just as he and Abbey had done that other night when snow was coming down in buckets.

"Greta, want to go outside and make snow angels?"

"Right now, Grandpa?"

"Right now, Greta!"

No effort was needed to convince her.

"Leave your pajamas on. They're good and warm. I bet we can find some socks in the dryer."

"I'll wear my pink cowgirl snowsuit."

"Don't forget a scarf and mittens and zip your boots all the way up."

"I will, Grandpa! I will."

They were ready in no time.

"Shh," motioned Steve, pulling the back door open. "We don't want anyone spoiling our fun."

"I'll be quiet, Grandpa."

Taking hold of Greta's hand, Steve led her through the porch and out the back door into a winter wonderland. The snow had let up some, allowing the moon to peek through the clouds. Stars were peeking as well. When the clouds stayed away long enough, a brilliance turned snowdrifts into beds of diamonds. Getting his bearings, going back to the night he and Abbey snuck out to play in the snow, Steve sought the spot where they'd made their snow angels.

"That's it," he said. "That's it, closer to the barn. That field is immense. The snow is untouched."

Because the snow was deep in most places, Steve carried Greta. Once they were situated, Steve reminded her about a few things.

"You've made snow angels before. Remember to plant your boots firmly in the snow and then drop back without catching yourself with your hands. It sounds hard but it isn't."

"I can do that, Grandpa. Daddy always tells me I make really nice snow angels."

As she was shutting her eyes and getting prepared, Greta jumped up and down.

"Grandpa! I have to go upstairs in the barn."

"Right now? Can't it wait until morning?"

"No. I have to go get something right now, Grandpa."

Sensing this was important, Steve picked her up. Into the barn they went. Reaching the narrow stairway, Greta asked her grandfather to wait for her. Steve didn't argue. He had a feeling this was out of his control.

Steve watched as she went up the stairs. He heard the light being turned on and the lid of the trunk opening and closing. Then she was coming back down the stairs.

"Are we good to go, honey?"

"Yes, Grandpa. It is time."

Steve noted Greta's serious tone. If she was trying to be dramatic, she'd succeeded. Carrying his granddaughter once again to that place in the field, they prepared to make snow angels and again Greta hesitated.

"Wait, Grandpa. Wait!"

Greta kept falling as she trudged through snowdrifts. It didn't stop her even when she tripped over her boots and fell face-first into the snow. Steve was about to rush to help her but something told him to stay put. He kept watch as she kept going. After a few more steps, she stopped. Looking up, Greta paused. Steve thought he saw her wipe her eyes, but it was hard to see with clouds getting in the way. As Greta reached into her pocket, the moon made its way out of the darkness. Steve could see her bending over and putting something in the snow. He couldn't make out what it was. It was too small. Stepping back, Greta looked up and then turned around and headed back. When she reached her grandfather, she took a deep breath. Planting her boots in the snow, Greta fell like a pro into the field of white.

"Wait for me, Greta!"

As Steve readied himself, he remembered the last time he'd made snow angels.

"We need to be farther apart," Abbey told him. "That's good, honey. Try not to catch yourself with your hands."

This time, with Greta nearby, Steve once again did as Abbey had instructed.

"What do you think, Greta? I didn't put my hands out. I'm ready to be a snow angel. On three, let's start moving our arms up and down. Then if you want, we can make another and another."

Greta didn't reply. She didn't move her arms.

"Are you okay? You must be tired. I think we should go in."

"No, Grandpa. I want to stay here."

"You're not tired?"

"No. I'm waiting."

Steve stayed still in his bed of snow. Afraid Greta might catch cold, a few minutes later he told her it was time to leave.

"Listen, Grandpa. Listen."

Steve did as she asked. He listened. He kept listening. A train was passing by in the distance but a train always did that at this particular time. About to get up, something stopped Steve like a ton of bricks. It sounded like violins, like harps being played and a chorus singing from somewhere deep within the woods. It didn't seem to get louder. It didn't seem to get closer. It was out there somewhere amidst the trees, out there where faith and belief take hold.

"Watch, Grandpa," said Greta now sitting up.

Steve sat up as well. Holding Greta's hand, they watched as wonder filled the night. It started with one candle, the simple white candle Greta had placed in the snow. As violins and harps kept playing, the candle was lit. Not by Greta. Not by Steve. It was lit by those notes of hope and joy. As that single candle flickered in the snow, another candle appeared. It too was lit. It too flickered. Then another and another candle appeared. Candles flickering in the untouched snow on this astounding night spread out as far as two snow angels could see. With the moon and stars now owning the heavens, it was a magical moment.

"Your grandmother gave you the candle, didn't she sweetheart?"

"Yes, Grandma is the candle giver. She left it in the trunk wrapped in paper. She told me to save it for a winter's night. It couldn't be just any winter night. Grandma said it had to be 'a wondrous night with fresh snow, a perfect winter night for snow angels.' She also told me you were her snow angel."

As hard as he tried, Steve couldn't hold back the tears. He'd asked Abbey for a sign. He couldn't go on in any relationship without knowing Abbey felt the same as when she'd written him that letter. He needed more, and the candle giver replied with a chorus from heaven, with harps and violins out among the trees and a resounding message of eternal love expressed in candles flickering in the snow.

"*Although I leave you, I'm going nowhere. Although I'm silent, you'll hear me whisper through the trees. Do not grieve, my darling. Laugh and love. Share and go on because I am in the wind and snow.*"

Hugging her grandfather, Greta jumped up and trudged through the drifts to that single candle. Holding it close, she went back and handed it to Steve.

"Grandpa, this is for you. Grandma asked me to give it to you."

Any doubt Steve had about taking that step had been answered. Was the result guaranteed? It never is. But because Steve was moving forward, he'd be stepping back into living.

"Can I make a snow angel, Grandpa?

"I'll make one right beside you."

With both of them making a perfect landing and moving their arms up and down, creating perfect wings, the two snow angels stayed there for a while as snow started falling again. They tried to count the snow-flakes floating down, but they couldn't keep up.

"I love winter, Grandpa."

"I'm not surprised, sweetheart."

Later, with Greta sound asleep, Steve turned the tree lights out and went upstairs. He put the white candle beside the wooden box with flowers painted all around it inside the top drawer of his nightstand. Sitting at the edge of his bed, watching glistening snowflakes fall, Steve noticed a sudden brightness coming from somewhere among the stars and snow. He knew it wasn't the shimmering moon. He knew as the brightness intensified he'd see colorful sparkles swirling over the land. Between the snow falling and the moon dancing, it was a sight fitting this night of miracles. Steve's attention turned to the barn, as lit up—as spectacular as ever.

Without hesitating, Steve was down the back stairs and out the kitchen door with no coat, boots, or scarf. Even with the snow swirling about his face, he wasn't cold. Closer to the barn, Steve noted the lantern up high in a window. When he reached the barn, he didn't have to open the door. To his surprise, Thomas was waiting for him. For a second they stood and stared at each other and then embraced.

Chapter Thirty-Five

"I didn't mean to startle you, Mr. Steve."

"On my way down here, I was thinking how strange it was going to be not having you here tonight."

"I was thinking the same thing, Mr. Steve, especially after all that happened last Christmas Eve. That's why I came ahead of Santa. I wanted to be at the door to greet you."

"I'll never forget inching along that window ledge in the snowstorm." Steve laughed, shutting the door and following Thomas through the barn to the reindeer stall.

"No storms in tonight's forecast. Santa will be on time."

"Any surprises this year?"

"Christmas is full of surprises, Mr. Steve, especially when you follow your heart."

Steve knew what Thomas was saying. His heart was singing.

The reindeer were restless. With a most splendid tree decorated in wild berries and acorns and with fresh boughs of cedar and pine wrapped about wooden posts and wreaths hung in front of windows up high, the reindeer knew this was the night. Motioning for Steve to stand with him by the tree, Thomas watched as the reindeer keeper approached the back of the stall. Taking a last look about, Edmund slid the latch up and then pushed with all his might. As he did, they could hear the ringing bells.

Swirls of crystals intensified. Steve could see the stars. They seemed so low as if about to touch the earth. Stirring snow filled the night air. The jingling of bells stopped.

A hush blanketed the night as Santa Claus stepped into the barn, followed by elves in a hurry carrying packages and trays of cookies. After spending time with the reindeer, Santa made his selections. Pointing to one and then another, the reindeer were taken outside and hitched to the sleigh. When the reindeer were in place, Santa left the barn with Edmund by his side.

"Is he leaving?"

"I told you Christmas is full of surprises, Mr. Steve."

Thomas didn't budge so Steve stayed put as well. Seconds later, shimmering snowflakes and dancing crystals blew in with the wind as the door opened and Santa stepped back inside. But he hesitated. Even though the wind was blowing, it was quiet. Anticipation does that. Anticipation brings wonder. This time, anticipation brought Edmund over to join Santa who was leading a chestnut brown pony into the barn.

Quiet remained as Santa and Edmund walked over to where Thomas and Steve were standing and staring in disbelief at a pony with a star on its forehead and a spirit to its gait.

"Edmund told me about the project you've been working on Steve. I felt this little beauty would add to the surprise tomorrow morning."

"But how did you . . . where did this pony come from, Santa?"

"She is from the North Pole. We have other animals besides reindeer back home."

"It is a beauty for sure," said Thomas.

"Greta will be ecstatic."

"I'd like to see what you've been working on. Then I must get going."

Steve led everyone through the barn.

"The last coat of paint was applied yesterday."

Opening the door to his workshop, Steve wasted no time pulling on an oversized tarp and letting it drop to the floor. There, amid odd pieces of wood and hammers and nails, sat a cutter. It was strawberry-red with a soft, pink cushioned seat and two, shiny black reins and brass bells.

Steve explained he got the idea when visiting Ben.

"I noticed a cutter that needed fixing sitting inside his carriage house. The cutter belonged to Henry. Ben explained how his father had been going a little too fast and took a corner too wide. I liked the size of the cutter. I thought it would be perfect for Greta."

"I can't imagine Mr. Henry going too fast," joked Thomas.

"That reminds me, Steve. I was pleased when learning you chose Henry to succeed you in your role here in the barn. He has earned that honor."

"That's what I concluded, Santa. Reading letters he'd written you when a little boy only confirmed my decision."

Taking a closer look at the cutter, Santa suggested Steve continue with more projects.

"Your craftsmanship is excellent."

"Thank you. Once I made up my mind that a cutter was my goal, it fell into place."

"Making up one's mind is the first step, Mr. Steve," said Thomas with a wink in his eye.

"It most certainly is."

On their way back to the stall, Edmund pointed out to Santa where the pony would be kept. "I'll freshen up the hay and fill the trough with water before bedding the pony down for the night."

As they walked back into the stall, Edmund and Steve figured out how they would surprise Greta in the morning. Then Edmund spent a little time with his family. Thomas passed the trays of cookies around. It wasn't long before Santa stood, announcing it was time to continue the journey.

"Merry Christmas, Steve. I'll be anxious to hear how Greta and her pony are getting along."

"Merry Christmas, Santa. Merry Christmas."

With the wind whispering and lanterns showing him the way, Santa and his team of reindeer were soon soaring above the earth. Once they were out of sight, Steve turned around. Thomas was not there. Steve was not surprised. He knew they'd see each other again. Saying good-night to Edmund, Steve started back home, trudging through the sparkling snow.

But Steve never did make it home. Instead, he was driving down Route 93, following his heart on this the most magical eve.

Chapter Thirty-Six

DESPITE THE HOUR, STEVE KNEW THIS was the moment. Eric had told him to stay vigilant. Thomas told him to follow his heart. Abbey's wish for Steve was for him to find happiness again. In her own way, she'd lit that path with the gift of a single candle. That path was leading Steve to the Quaker-style home with a cranberry door. From a conversation over coffee a few weeks back, Steve knew Susan was home. He knew she'd be leaving for Maine again right after Christmas. If he didn't speak up now, Steve realized that path would lead nowhere.

The glorious wonder of Christmas swirled about the pine trees and around the white fence almost invisible against the snow. Small lights framing the door twinkled in the cold. Lights were still on inside. Walking up the few front steps, Steve took a deep breath and rang the bell. So many thoughts went flashing through his mind as he stood there, waiting. From a dance in the school gym to making snow angels, it all came at him in an instant.

Sometimes we find ourselves at a crossroads we never imagined. Life does that. The trick is to stay resolute. There is a plan for each of us. Getting there requires believing.

After a few minutes, Steve knocked on the door. He called out her name.

"Susan. It's me. It's Steve. I have to—"

The door opened. Wrapped in a soft, pink robe that fell to the floor, with her hair free and her eyes enhanced by the twinkling lights, Susan's smile put Steve at rest. "Is something wrong, Steve?"

"No. Nothing is wrong, Susan. I need . . . we need to talk."

"Right now?"

"Yes. Right now, if you don't mind my barging in uninvited."

Pulling the door wide open, Susan reminded Steve he was always welcome. "Pardon the mess. I'm in the middle of packing. Would you like a cup of coffee? Some tea?" Taking a closer look at Steve as he stood in the hallway, Susan made another suggestion. "I'm in the mood for an old-fashioned hot toddy."

"That sounds perfect."

As they passed through the dining room to the kitchen, Steve noticed the little ceramic tree on the table.

"I turn it on every evening. It was such a thoughtful gift."

They made small talk as Susan mixed whiskey with hot water. Once she added everything, including a cinnamon stick, they went in by the fire.

"I usually end up here late at night. There's a feel to this room that soothes me."

"I understand what you mean. Many a night I fall asleep in my chair. Abbey used to tease me, telling me I got the best sleep in the front room."

The clock on the mantle announced it was Christmas. Taking a sip of his toddy, Steve looked into those green eyes warming his heart. "May I be the first to wish you Merry Christmas."

"Merry Christmas, Steve. I'm happy you are here."

"You are?"

"Yes. Why would you question that?"

"I feel like a fool knocking at your door at such a late hour, but I haven't been able—I haven't been able to stop thinking about you. Forgive me if I'm talking out of place, but I feel I have to speak up before you go back to him."

"Him?"

Trying to keep his thoughts from coming out in more of a jumbled mess than they already were, Steve stopped for a moment. Taking a drink while never taking his eyes off Susan, Steve reached over and moved strands of that silky, mahogany hair off her shoulders—brushing his fingers along the nap of her neck.

Both were taken back by the touch. Susan set her glass down. Standing, she walked over to the fireplace. Stirring the coals, she explained how Paul had been the one to build the fires and keep them going. Susan stayed put watching the flames—listening to the logs crackle. Taking a deep breath as if gathering her thoughts, she went back to the sofa. Picking up her drink, Susan again questioned Steve who he was referring to when saying 'him.'

"That man with the purple tie and a beard. The artsy-looking fellow."

"I'm afraid I don't know what you are talking about."

"Last February a woman who said she was a friend of yours living in Portland called to tell me about an art event taking place in your honor. She'd heard you mention my name a few times and thought I might be interested in surprising you by attending."

Susan sat still, listening to Steve talk nonstop.

"So I did."

"You did what?"

"I drove to Portland. I was in the crowd of people standing and clapping when you came into that ballroom looking so beautiful on the arm of that guy dressed in an expensive suit and fancy tie."

"That's the purple tie you were referring to?"

"Yes."

"So what did you do after we came into the room?"

"I stood there watching you embrace your fellow artists. I stood there as he kissed you. That's when I realized I didn't fit in. I'm not the artsy type."

"I need to refresh my drink."

Susan got up and walked towards the kitchen. Steve followed.

"I'll take a refresher as well."

"Now it all adds up. Since returning from Maine, you've seemed distant. I couldn't figure out why. You have to realize I am not the artsy type either. Here. Try this."

"But you're an artist," replied Steve testing his drink. "You looked so comfortable. I assumed you were enjoying yourself."

"You assumed wrong. Attending events like that is part of being an artist. You have to mingle. You have to play in the right circles but that doesn't mean I enjoy the mingling and playing. I prefer creating in the silence of my studio. I prefer being surrounded by paints and brushes and canvas and wind blowing and inspiration flowing."

"But he kissed you."

After stirring her drink a little more, Susan went back to the front room. When Steve was sitting next to her, she continued.

"That guy I was with is Phillip—my agent—a flamboyant Italian. He wears his heart on his sleeve. We've been together since art school. He does all my publicity, and as you witnessed, he enjoys every minute of it."

"He had me convinced."

"Phillip is like that even in down times. Fact is he's able to get my art in places I'd never be able to even get an appointment. There's more to being an artist than the creating."

"I understand, Susan. It's a business."

"Exactly. Phillip takes over where I am the weakest. He gets my artwork and that ignites that passion of his."

"I feel like a fool, reacting as I did."

Something in the tone of Steve's voice made Susan realize what was truly bothering him. It had nothing to do with Phillip or her artwork. Going up to the mantle, she brought back candles in crystal holders. After lighting them, Susan placed them on a coffee table explaining, "We need a touch of Christmas."

"I'm overwhelmed you drove all that way to support me." Susan continued. "I wish I'd known you were in that mass of people. Of all the ones who were there, having you present if only for a short period of time means the most to me."

Looking into those green eyes glistening in the candlelight, Steve admitted he wished he'd stayed.

"You didn't drive back that night, did you?"

"No. I went next door and had some seafood and a few beers."

"Oh, I would have enjoyed that so much more."

"Really?"

The wind knocking against French doors distracted Steve. He didn't hear Susan's question so she repeated it.

"Why do you continue not to believe me?"

"I'm not good at this."

"At what?"

Finishing his drink, Steve got up the courage to explain. "Abbey and I had been together since high school. The thought of starting over has been overwhelming since losing her."

Susan stayed quiet for a few minutes. Then turning, she moved closer to Steve. As the logs crackled and the candle flickered, Susan held Steve's hand.

"I understand what you mean by being overwhelmed. When I lost Paul, I convinced myself that my life from that point on would be my art and my children. You've helped me realize I was protecting myself. I was choosing to retreat from life rather than put myself in a position of possible rejection. That thinking fell apart the evening we ran into each other. There was something about you, Steve. You were the one standing out in a crowd. I remember coming home realizing I wanted to feel again. You have awakened me, Steve. I feel alive."

"That's it, Susan. That's the turning point when dealing with grief. It's getting past the sorrow and guilt and realizing you want to feel again."

Far off in the distance, the wail of the train that passed by like clockwork sent its soulful song over treetops and fields as muted lights of the season swayed in the night.

With tears falling, Susan held Steve's hand even tighter. "I've been waiting for you to come to me, Steve."

"I'm here, Susan. You've gotten to me. I want to stay the night. I want to lie beside you and hear the wind blow and watch the snow fall. I want to wake up beside you now and forever. I love you, Susan. I give you my heart."

"I want you to stay the night. I want to wake up beside you now and forever, Steve. My love is yours for all eternity."

Taking Susan's glass, Steve put it down on the table next to his.

Turning around, brushing strands of hair back from her eyes with his fingers, Steve kissed away tears, one by one. Pushing her robe down off her shoulders, Steve kissed her neck, softly and repeatedly, while whispering in her ear. Then gently, ever so gently, Steve moved his lips to hers. As passions grew, Susan led Steve upstairs. Two who thought they'd never feel love again felt rapture ignite as the wind kept blowing and snowflakes kept falling.

Steve made it home a little before 5:30 a.m. He thought he'd get back before anyone was awake. To his surprise, Eric was in the kitchen, rolling out dough. He told his father the coffee would be ready when he came back downstairs.

Chapter Thirty-Seven

A FEW HOURS LATER, THE OLD farmhouse was wide awake. Greta and Bobby checked to make sure Santa had eaten his snack.

"All the sugar's gone too," said Greta. "The reindeer were hungry."

"I hope you're hungry," said Eric. "I remember how much you loved Sophie's jam tarts. I made some this morning."

"Pancakes, too, Daddy?"

"Pancakes and French toast as well, honey."

Steve was the last to come downstairs. Eric had his coffee ready.

"Black with a touch of sugar."

"Perfect. Thanks, Eric. Merry Christmas everyone."

Looking at Greta, he added. "I wonder if Santa stopped last night."

"He did, Grandpa! My stocking is full and he left me presents!"

"Breakfast is ready."

"Then we can open presents, Daddy?"

"Yes. Then you can open presents."

While walking into the dining room, Steve told Greta sometimes a present is too big to wrap.

"Like the one you made me out in the barn?"

"Why do you think what I was making is for you?"

"You'd always smile when you told me not to go in that room, Grandpa."

Candles were lit. China used for as long as anyone could remember was in place. Family gathered sat down to share the moment.

Sammy asked Steve if Edmund would be stopping by.

"He said he would."

"He's doing a good job since replacing his father?"

"Edmund is his father's son," said Steve.

"Will we be seeing Susan at some point?" asked Eric.

"Susan is coming for dinner."

"That's wonderful," said Meg. "We haven't seen her in such a long time."

"You'll be seeing more of her in the future, Meg." That was all Steve offered. Eric changed the subject.

"I must say, Elizabeth, having you here on Christmas morning is a long-awaited gift."

"Thank you. I feel blessed being here with Meg, with all of you."

"I love coming home for Christmas," said Sammy. "I always find great story lines."

"How's Greta and Miracle's story coming?" asked Steve.

"It's moving along," said Sammy, not wanting to spill the beans about a certain gift under the tree.

"I still miss Miracle."

"I'm sure he misses you," said Meg.

"I thought Santa would bring me a pony."

"Did you ask him for a pony?"

"I put a pony on my list in my letter, Grandpa."

Breakfast lasted longer than usual for a Christmas morning. Conversation jumped from documentaries to the story behind the jam tarts and back to Miracle again. Once they got up from the table, dishes were cleared and more coffee was made. Elizabeth took the little ones into the front room. Soon they were all gathered around the tree with the angel on top.

Bobby and Greta opened surprises stuffed inside their stockings. Then the attention went to the gifts. There were so many gifts under that tree. One by one they ripped them open. Greta didn't understand her present from Sammy. Once he explained, Greta ran over and gave him a hug. She couldn't talk. She was crying.

"Grandpa told me he cries happy tears sometimes. You made me happy, Uncle Sammy."

With the last of the gifts opened, Bobby and Greta were taking a closer look at what they'd received when a knock at the back door caught Eric's attention. It was Edmund, asking for help down at the barn.

"I don't want to alarm everyone, but I need all the help I can get!"

Without hesitating, everyone stopped what they were doing and hurried to grab their coats and boots. Scarves and gloves were sought. Even Elizabeth and Bobby followed Edmund out the door. No one said a word. Everyone was worried as they rushed into the barn.

"It's coming from in there. I keep hearing something moving inside your work space, Mr. Steve."

"Move out of the way, everyone. Sammy, Eric, follow me."

The plan was working. Everyone stayed back while the three slowly opened the door. Steve whispered to his sons not to react.

"Looks like whatever it was has gone, Edmund. There is something that needs explaining, though."

Opening the door for all to see, he revealed more excitement on that Christmas morning.

"Santa brought me my pony," squealed Greta, so enthralled with the pony that she didn't notice the cutter until Meg pointed it out.

"Oh, Grandpa! I love my cutter! It has a pink seat! Thank you, Grandpa! Thank you! I am so happy! I have a pony, Bobby. Look, isn't she pretty! Santa brought me my pony. I hope the wild horses come and see her!"

"I'm certain the wild horses already know your pony is here, Miss Greta. They'll never forget what you did for Miracle."

If ever a Christmas morning kept bringing one gift of joy after another, this was that morning. Greta stayed in the barn with Edmund and her pony while everyone went to the cemetery. The two added fresh hay on top of the fresh hay Edmund had already put in her stall. They filled a trough with water. Edmund found a brush Greta would be able to use when her pony was a little older. Greta stayed into the afternoon until Edmund asked about her grandmother's wooden box—the one she'd painted flowers on when she was a little girl. "My father told me about it. I would love to see it sometime."

"Do you like flowers?"

"I do, Miss Greta."

Thinking about that wooden box gave Greta an idea. She kept thinking about it while watching her pony sleep. She tried not to think about it but the idea kept getting better and better. Finally she tiptoed out of the stall. "I have to go home, Edmund. Please take good care of my pony."

Looking at her new friend brushing a reindeer, Greta asked Edmund to dinner. "I will help you with your chores later."

"You do not have to help me, Miss Greta. Thank you for the invitation. I will be happy to join you and your family for dinner."

Greta skipped through the snow all the way back to the farmhouse.

Chapter Thirty-Eight

ERIC WAS BACK IN THE KITCHEN working on yet another dinner. Meg had asked earlier if he was getting tired of coming up with one spectacular meal after another. Eric reminded her how the kitchen was his studio.

"Paint brushes or recipes—they are one and the same to me."

Meg understood. She saw him come alive when cooking. That's what he was doing when Greta came barreling through the back door.

"Daddy! I asked Edmund to come to dinner. And he said yes! Where's Grandpa?"

Eric was curious as to why she asked where her grandfather was and why she ran through the kitchen and up the stairs when learning Steve had gone to Susan's some time ago. When she came back down, Greta didn't stop. She went right out the door.

"Was that Greta?"

"That was our daughter, honey. She is up to something."

"It probably involves her pony. I was as surprised as she was this morning. Did Steve mention anything to you about getting Greta a pony?"

"No. He kept that secret just as he did the cutter. I loved the story Dad told on the way to the cemetery about how Henry's cutter was the inspiration."

"Mom did too. I hope she'll meet Henry and Sophie at some point."

"I'm sure that will happen, Meg. I have a feeling your mother might surprise you and move closer."

"When we were kneeling in front of Abbey's gravesite, Mom told Abbey she was the reason we were no longer strangers."

"Funny how things work out if we wait long enough. Thanks to Mom, going to the cemetery has become tradition. Besides the poinsettias and wreaths we left on the tombstones, another part of that tradition has been the sleigh full of people passing by out in the field. It was comforting to see them there again, with their scarves flying in the wind, being pulled by the same two horses. They've become part of our Christmas in a way they will never know."

WHEN STEVE AND SUSAN ARRIVED, EVERYONE gathered by the tree. Eric had the fire going. He and Meg carried in silver trays holding the long-stemmed crystal glasses they brought out every Christmas with choices of wine or eggnog. Sammy had music playing in the background as snowflakes whispered past the windows. Once the drinks were poured, Meg went back to the kitchen for trays of hors d'oeuvres prepared at the restaurant. Greta helped her mother carry them in to the front room.

"Your grandfather told me Santa brought you a pony, Greta."

"She's a beautiful pony with a diamond."

"I had a pony when I was a little girl."

"Did your pony have a diamond?"

"No, my pony did not have a diamond. I think Santa brought you a very special pony. Have you given your pony a name?"

"Her name is Rosy."

"Why did you call her Rosy?"

"My grandma drew me a picture of a pony. Mommy said she had rosy cheeks. She was very pretty just like my new pony. Do you want to go see Rosy after we eat?"

"I would love to see Rosy."

"Good." Greta smiled and ran to play with Bobby.

"The tree is beautiful," said Susan.

"It's all Meg's work," said Eric.

"Did you put a tree up, Susan?"

"We always had a real tree when the kids were little. Thanks to Steve, I now have a beautiful little ceramic tree sitting on my dining-room table."

"That's all you need especially if you're leaving for Maine," said Eric.

"I plan on leaving in a few weeks."

"Are you flying or driving?"

Steve took hold of Susan's hand and answered Eric's question. "I am going to drive Susan to Maine. We'll be staying through March."

Funny how a few words can change everything. Funny how those few words mean so much more. It was apparent to Eric his father had gotten beyond his funk.

"That's great, Dad," said Sammy. "Watch out Susan. He'll have you eating seafood for breakfast!"

"As long as your father does the cooking, that's fine with me!"

"He's a great cook when he has to be," said Eric. "I'm happy you're going, Dad."

"Thanks boys. We spoke with Ben and Ellie earlier. They're joining us at some point. Ben wants to take us on a road trip through New Hampshire. They said they'd call back later after Henry and Sophie—Julian and his girls get there for dinner."

"I've always wanted to wander through New Hampshire," said Cate.

"They've done it for years," said Steve, pausing before adding, "And, there's one more thing."

Steve hesitated. Clearing his throat, he explained.

"When we return in the spring, Susan and I will be husband and wife."

Once again that old farmhouse—surrounded by fields and pine trees with that majestic barn full of horses, and sheep and glorious reindeer set off in a field with snow angels resting nearby—erupted with joy. Steve filled everyone in on their plans made in the wee hours of the morning.

"Both of us lost the loves of our lives. We've talked in depth about Abbey and Paul. They will forever be a part of our journey. Neither of us thought we'd ever get beyond the grief to a point of finding love again. But we have."

Holding Susan's hand even tighter while wiping away tears welling in his eyes, Steve continued. "It will be a simple ceremony in an old chapel in Portland by the bay. The reception will be held at Susan's home. I'd like you, Eric and you, Sammy to be my best men."

Eric and Sammy were the first to congratulate the couple.

"Mom would be so happy for you, Dad," said Eric.

"Welcome to the family, Susan. You've put a smile back on Dad's face."

"Your father has put a smile in my heart, Sammy. We are blessed to have found each other."

Eric excused himself. Someone was knocking at the back door.

"Welcome, Edmund. Your timing is perfect."

When Eric told him the news, Edmund grinned from one little ear to the other. He walked into the front room and shook Steve's hand.

"I will be certain to tell my father and his friend the good news, Mr. Steve."

"Thank you, Edmund."

FOLLOWING STEVE AND SUSAN INTO THE dining room, Greta took her place at the table beside her mother. Then she waited. She didn't have to wait long.

"Where did that beautiful centerpiece come from?"

"I made it, Daddy," said Greta, while looking at her grandfather. "I wanted it to be special. This is a very special dinner. I have a new pony and now Grandpa has a new friend."

Steve was overwhelmed by Greta's creation sitting in the middle of a table that had welcomed so many for so many Christmases. Fresh pine boughs surrounded a wooden box with flowers painted on it long ago by a mother and her little girl. Inside the wooden box sat a snowman with different color mittens, hand-sewn by the snowman maker. Next to the precious snowman was a simple white candle left inside a trunk by the candle giver for a grandchild she'd never know. Because of the candle giver's letter and that white candle found and placed in the snow, lighting a winter's night with reassurance, Steve would be moving on while keeping that candle giver forever in his heart. Witnessing the moment was the reindeer keeper—son of Thomas—friend of Santa—caretaker of fields and pastures and barns immersed in tradition—steward of majestic reindeer responsible for that most wondrous Christmas Eve flight. Believing sings its song to young and old alike. If you believe—that song will forever sing its magic in your heart.

Do not grieve, my darling. Laugh and love. Share and go on, because I am in the wind and snow. I'll blossom in the flowers. I'll spread my wings and reach beyond the mountaintops.

Some things truly are meant to be.

BARBARA BRIGGS WARD is a writer who lives in Ogdensburg, New York. She is author of the award-winning Christmas story, *The Reindeer Keeper*, released October 2010 and selected by both Yahoo's Christmas Book Club and Yonkers, NY Riverfront Library Book Club as their December, 2012 featured book of the month.

Barbara followed with the release of *The Snowman Maker* in October 2013. Her articles and short stories have appeared in the Chicken Soup for the Soul book, *Christmas Magic*; the Chicken Soup for the Soul book, *Family Caregivers*; *Ladies' Home Journal*; *The Crafts Report, Highlights for Children,* and *The Saturday Evening Post* online. Her projects include creator of the Snarly Sally book series.

Barbara has been a featured writer on Mountain Lake PBS in Plattsburgh, New York and at Target Book Festivals in Boston and New York .

Barbara invites you to visit www.barbarabriggsward.com.

SUZANNE LANGELIER-LEBEDA is an award-winning graphic designer and fine artist from northern New York, living on the Raquette River at the edge of the Adirondack Park.

She earned BS and MFA degrees from Buffalo State (including study in Siena, Italy) and Rochester Institute of Technology. After working as a designer at SUNY (State University of New York) Geneseo, and City University New York, she returned home to SUNY Potsdam as a graphic designer and director/designer in publications.

She designed and produced primarily admissions and development materials for the college, often enhanced by her illustrations. She left in

2000 to concentrate on freelance graphic design, illustration and her personal fine art.

Website: suzannelebeda.com

She is an exhibiting member of the Adirondack Artists Guild in Saranac Lake, NY. Her solo show of drawings, Re*Imagine, opened September, 2015 at The Artists Guild.